fragile

WILD HARE
COLLECTIVE

Copyright © 2017 by Jandra Sutton

First Printing, 2017

ISBN 978-0-692-90631-6

Wild Hare Collective
Nashville, TN 37214

www.wildharecollective.com

Printed in the United States of America

For Bryan

PROLOGUE

Do you ever wonder what it's like to be deaf?

To see the world buzzing to life around you, to see colors and faces and a swirl of activity that you can feel, taste, touch, smell, but hear...nothing?

You might think it sounds like a horrible thing. Trapped inside your own mind, unable to communicate or express yourself. To be without the ability to hear, surely, would be awful. No music, no movies, no phone calls.

Maybe you feel bad for those who cannot hear. You know what they're missing, after all, because that's exactly it. They're missing something. They're lacking. They're impaired.

What if you are wrong?

What if being deaf presented you with the opportunity to see the world through an entirely unique lens? Instead of missing something, you've gained something different. The ability to see what others might not. The chance to experience life and all of its challenges in a way that a majority of the world will never even begin to imagine.

Deaf doesn't mean 'broken'.
Deaf means different.

CHAPTER 1

High school sucked.

Ask any typical American teenager and he or she would tell you the truth. That is unless, of course, he or she was either A) deluded B) lying or C) popular.

For me, Ava Collins, high school was just a means to an end. It wasn't fun, it wasn't about the parties, and - yes - it most definitely sucked.

Why?

The answer to that question was fairly simple. High school sucked because people sucked.

Starting at 7:50 AM every morning, I was subjected to a series of torturous interactions with the people I hated to admit were my peers.

Today was no different.

First period flew by without a hitch. It normally does, considering it's study hall. Ah, study hall. The one high school class it's impossible to fail. Completely stress-free, most of the students in my study hall at Lincoln High School chose to utilize their free time to catch up on the sleep they didn't get the night before. They were probably partying, getting wasted, or hooking up. Not that I'd know. My classmates practically belonged to another species.

Right off the bat in second period, however, the day inevitably took a turn for the worse. The class was assigned two chapters to study and answer the accompanying thirty-six questions in their Advanced Placement biology textbooks. Our teacher, Mr. Rutger, preferred to take the 'hands-off' approach to learning. Most of the class involved taking down notes and countless worksheets, sprinkled with the occasional dissection...which was actually *optional*.

Who decided to make dissection optional in biology? Didn't it defeat the whole purpose of the class? More to the point, how were students supposed to pass an AP biology exam with a teacher who doesn't actually teach?

You might have thought, "Wow. An entire forty-five-minute class to work on thirty-six questions. That doesn't sound too bad."

Well, you would be wrong. Each question required a well-thought-out paragraph for an answer, and - with thirty-six questions multiplied by at least 5 to 10 minutes per question - that added up to a lot of biology homework.

Lucky for the class, Mr. Rutger wasn't that much of a sucker for torture. Partners were almost always allowed, which cut the workload (and the misery) in half.

Except for me.

Why? Because no one wanted to work with the deaf girl.

It wasn't like I couldn't do the work. I'm not mute or anything, but - unfortunately - most of my classmates were under the impression that just because I can't hear them, I can't communicate.

They were oh-so-wrong.

I'm loud. Probably the most outgoing and talkative girl in the senior class, but - thanks to bullies - I learned early on to keep quiet and stick in the corner. I mean, I'm not *loud*, loud. Not verbally, but I'm definitely not afraid to make my opinion known either.

Ninety-nine percent of the people I've encountered, however, just weren't able to understand me when I did.

Today, I just bit back a sigh and started working on the assignment. There wasn't any point in looking around for a partner, and - to be frank - I was pretty okay with that anyway. People sucked, remember? At least this way I knew I'd get an A.

When the bell rang, students flooded out of the classroom, and I took my time. Why rush to get into the hallway when I was just going to crushed by the swarm of bodies? It wasn't exactly fun to navigate the halls of my high school when I can't hear what was going on around me. Sure, it's not hard, but have you ever thought about what it's like to hear a group of teen boys thunder down the hallway behind you? You get out of the way, right?

For me, that was a little more difficult. I could feel the movement in the floor beneath my feet, and I always tried to pay attention to the faces of everyone around me. If people were coming, someone was bound to look over a shoulder at them. I always had to be 'on' during the day, focusing on the faces - on the sensations around me - and never able to just...exist. It was doable, definitely, and but if I was completely honest with myself, I had to admit that it was sometimes exhausting.

Today was one of those days. The kind of day where the world was already catching up with me, and I'd give anything to go back home, climb into bed, and press reset. I could practically taste the ice cream that waited for me in the freezer at home, and my heart yearned for a good, old-fashioned Netflix binge.

I tossed my laptop into my back, followed by my textbook, and exited the classroom with a smile at my teacher. Mr. Rutger was nice, at least, even if he was a horrible teacher. After adjusting my bag over my shoulder, I turned to the right and narrowly avoided a collision with a large, man-shaped wall.

"Whoa!" Zach Kennedy said, swiftly sidestepping me. "Sorry, I--"

Glancing down, he froze when he realized who it was. The deaf chick. He didn't know sign language or any of that shit, so he just shrugged and walked away.

Because what use was an apology to a deaf person?

I clenched my fists, resisting the urge to shoot him a particular sign with my middle finger that everyone understood, and headed down the hallway to my next class.

Zach and his friends were the worst of my classmates. Some people at least tried to be polite, smiling and nodding at me in the hallways, but most seemed to prefer to believe that I was a persona non grata. Hell, I was practically invisible.

Everyone pretty much acted like I was. At lunch, in class, in the hallways - they wouldn't even bother talking behind my back because they thought they could get away with saying whatever shit they wanted to my face. Not like I could hear them, right?

Wrong. I've spent seventeen years learning how to lipread like a champ, meaning I was forced to suffer through endless teenage brutality - aka, stupidity - because people were stupid and forgot that just because I can't hear, that doesn't mean I can't think.

And, of course, it was only third period.

I wouldn't mind if someone were to kill me now.

CHAPTER 2

By the end of fourth period, I was seriously considering faking an illness to get out of the rest of the day at school. I have the same thought every day if I'm honest, but it's just a matter of when it pops up. Usually, I make it past lunch. Today was not one of those days.

I walked into the cafeteria late, as usual, and grabbed a turkey wrap. The lunch lady smiled at me as I punched in my student ID number to pay for the food, and I forced a friendly grin back at her.

Rebecca. Lunch lady Rebecca. She was one of the nicest people in the school, always giving me a friendly greeting no matter how shitty the day was for either of us. I couldn't help but wonder if she knew I was deaf, but somehow I don't think Rebecca would care. She'd give me the same smile no matter what. Basically, she represented the good in society for me. At least there was one decent person left in a world of assholes.

Good luck, Rebecca, with carrying that burden.

Being the only deaf kid in school meant that I spent a lot of time in solitude. No one ever expressed an interest in getting to know me - not since elementary school when I was some kind of novelty to the other kids - and most people seemed to think I was mute as well as deaf.

To a degree, I am. It's not that I can't speak, it's that I never had the opportunity to learn how. My vocal cords work, I assure you, but seeing how someone forms words is a lot different than hearing how those words should sound in real life. I used to try, but I gave up when kids would tease me for saying things wrong. My voice always sounded funny, and - like I said - people sucked.

I've been deaf since I was a baby. That's right, I could hear once upon a time. Not that I really remember what that was like. Born premature, I suffered permanent damage to my inner ear. Apparently, this was caused by a severe lack of oxygen when I was born. They used mechanical ventilation to help me breathe because my tiny little lungs couldn't expand on their own, and I spent a lot of time in neonatal intensive care.

Unfortunately, that wasn't the only problem I suffered. Nope, I just had to catch pneumonia. If you didn't know, infants already have a weakened immune system for the first year of life, which meant I was royally screwed. Once I recovered, thankfully, I was screened for hearing loss and my parents were given a checklist of things to 'look out for' should further hearing loss occur.

It did.

When I was 2 months old, I was diagnosed with progressive hearing loss. As I got older, my hearing continued to disintegrate, which was wonderful for my early life development as you can imagine. My parents tried hearing aids, but - by the time I was 2 years old - my hearing deteriorated to a point where my audiologist discovered that the hearing aids were no longer helping.

He suggested cochlear implants, which are tiny little electronic devices that would do what my damaged inner ear doesn't. Hearing aids just amplify sounds, but - if your inner ear can't pick up anything, no matter how loud it is - that doesn't really help. That's where the cochlear implant stepped in to save the day. It completely bypasses the damage in your inner ear and sends signals straight to your brain.

Pretty cool, huh?

Unluckily, my parents couldn't afford the procedure, which could run anywhere from $40,000 to $100,000. Their insurance wouldn't cover it either, meaning I was out of luck. However, my mom discovered that I was eligible for Medicaid and that - thanks to a new law in 2004 - Medicaid was required to cover cochlear implants. She was desperate to have a 'relatively normal' daughter, and she hated learning sign language, so she got me signed up for Medicaid. My dad, on the other hand, refused to consent to the surgery. He really didn't like the idea of his daughter going under the knife to have some doctors 'screw around with her head', as he put it, and my mom caved.

No cochlear implants for me.

My mom brought up the idea at least once a year since then, but my dad always refused. Instead, I went to special classes during elementary school that helped me learn ASL - American sign language - and my mom joined a playgroup where she went once a month to talk to other hearing moms of deaf children while the kids played. I liked it, and I made a few friends, but when my dad found out he pitched a fit.

He didn't want me to associate with other deaf kids because he didn't want to raise some kind of 'weirdo' who couldn't communicate with 'real people in the real world.' He was worried that I'd rely on sign language 24/7 instead of improving my lip reading skills, which he thought were more important for my survival. I'm pretty sure he expected my hearing to recover some day, as if it was something that could just...grow back, or he was holding out for doctors to invent some pill that would fix my 'problem', as he put it.

Remember how I said people suck? My dad sucks more. He's an asshole if you hadn't already noticed.

I'm not upset that I never got cochlear implants. To be honest, I'm not sure I would want them now. Being deaf was part of my identity, just like being blonde, having green eyes, or being absolutely terrible at kickball. I hated it when people apologized for my deafness like it meant I was less of a human being, because that's absolutely not the case. I had a normal childhood. I played tee-ball when I was little, went swimming at the lake with my cousins, obsessed over Harry Potter, and swooned over Sebastian Stan.

I never wanted apologies, I wanted to be treated like I was the same as everyone else. Lack of hearing didn't change that.

I mean, sure, I'm different, but who isn't? Does what make you different from everyone else make you less of a living, breathing human being?

Answer? No.

CHAPTER 3

I found an empty table near the corner of the cafeteria, and I sat down to eat my lunch. Fortunately, my deafness means I'm allowed to bring my laptop with me everywhere, so I flip open my computer and navigate to Twitter to check my notifications.

Surprised? You shouldn't be. I'm practically Twitter famous, and I've got over 10,000 followers from all over the world. I told you that I was loud. The internet provided me with the opportunity to be myself, to communicate clearly and have no one know (or care) that I couldn't hear. Plus, my tweets are pretty hilarious. Not that I'm biased or anything.

I pulled the plastic off my wrap and fired off a few quick replies to some of my messages before retweeting a few jokes. I pride myself in my ability to both create and share great content, and I love being accessible online. No one wants to talk to me in school, so I always make a point to respond to each and every person who talks to me on social media. I read in some marketing blog that people want to connect with people and that it's important to build your 'personal brand' in an engaging way that encourages interaction, so that's what I've done.

Halfway through my lunch, a shadow fell across my computer screen. I glanced over my shoulder just in time to see the devil, Zach Kennedy, as he plopped down into the seat next to me with a wicked grin on his face.

"Thanks for the food," he said, reaching over to grab the rest of my lunch and stuffing it into his mouth.

His friends circled the tables like vultures, and even though I couldn't hear them, I could see the cruel laughter written on their faces. Zach turned away from me, saying something that I couldn't understand without reading his lips, and the faces around the table lit up.

Zach the ass, always a comedian.

He grabbed my laptop next, still talking, but I reach out and attempt to tug it out of his hands. We struggled for a few seconds until he let go, holding his hands up in mock surrender, and said something else I couldn't quite catch.

Slamming the computer shut, I tucked it into my back before glaring back at Zach.

"Didn't know you were Twitter famous, freak," he said, moving his lips in an exaggeratedly slow fashion before he turned back to his friends to say something else.

I pushed my seat backward, slinging my backpack over one shoulder, and stood up to leave. Zach, unfortunately, decided to join me with his friends in tow. He walked backward ahead of me, drawing the attention of most of the cafeteria's occupants, as he laughed and talked at me. I barely caught what he said as I tried to get around him, but his friends made it impossible for me to dodge him.

"So what did you do to get so many followers, Ava?" Zach asked. "Some kind of deaf-girl porn? Didn't know people were into that, but - then again - I guess I can't knock it until I try it. I wouldn't mind giving it a shot with you sometime."

My eyes grew wide as I realized what he was saying, and a glance around the room confirmed that pretty much everyone was laughing with him. Of course they were. God, people sucked so much.

Slowing to a halt, I pulled out the tiny notepad I always carried with me in my back pocket and scribbled a note on it. My hands were itching to sign every insult known to mankind at him, along with a few snarky remarks, but I knew they would fall on deaf ears.

Ha. Look at me, I'm hilarious.

Instead, I folded up the paper and shoved it into Zach's chest. He laughed as he took it, allowing me to pass, before unfolding it and reading the message. I couldn't resist checking over my shoulder as he read the note, watching his expression as it changed from one of amusement to one of rage.

Sorry, but I wouldn't touch your dick with a ten-foot pole. Pretty sure Matt would take care of it for you though. Bet you'd enjoy that, asshat.

I waved at him cheerily before turning my hand over to give him the bird, and - before I could get away from him - his hand reached out and locked onto the strap of my backpack and pulled me backward. I toppled backward, losing my balance easily, and slammed into the floor. My head snapped back and smashed into the tile while the wind rushed out of my lungs. Above me, Zach and his friends panicked - all of them running in the opposite direction - while tears pricked in the corner of my eyes.

A tall figure appeared in front of me just as the bell rang. I could tell from the swarm of students rushing from the tables, their feet thundering on the floor beneath me, and I tried to sit up to avoid being crushed in the mass exodus. The guy in front of me shook his head, saying something I couldn't quite make out before he beckoned over a faculty member. His face looked familiar, but my head felt wonky and my vision was a bit too blurry to make anything out as I tried to prevent the onslaught of tears from pouring down my face.

Damn, I never wanted to cry in school. I hadn't since 7th grade when Tiffany Badecki slammed me into the lockers and accused me of 'looking at her funny.' Typically, I was pretty good at hiding my emotions around my peers. Don't let them know that they get to you and all that, but today...today just sucked ass. Not only did I let Zach get to me in the worst way, now I'm laying on the dirty cafeteria floor with tears cascading down my cheeks.

Ah, high school, thou art a heartless wench.

CHAPTER 4

I spent the next hour in the nurse's office arguing against calling my mother. Yes, she's my mom, and sure, she used to be a nurse, but I really didn't see the point in calling her up about something as silly as a bump on the head. The nurse kept saying something about a concussion, and she even found one of the ladies from the front office to 'translate' things to me. And by that, I mean finger spell. The only ASL she actually knew was how to sign the lyrics to Michael W. Smith's "Our God Is An Awesome God."

I lost my tiny notebook when I fell, which sucks because it would've made this situation a lot easier to handle. Plus, that notebook - while primarily used to communicate with my teachers - did contain a fair amount of private information. Here's hoping the janitors found it because I really don't want to worry about someone discovering that I drew a cartoon depicting my calculus teacher as a zombie who sucked out all of our brains.

Needless to say, I really don't like math.

After about ten minutes, the nurse finally realized that I was asking for pen and paper and brought me a notebook. I scribbled down some made up explanation about why we couldn't call my mom - that she was at work and not allowed to answer calls or something - which she seemed to accept.

"What about your dad?" She asked me.

Nope. No dad. Absolutely not. I wrote a simple 'NO' in capital letters on the paper, and the nurse sighed before sending the lady from the front office back to her desk.

"Honey," the nurse frowned. "You need to go to the emergency room. You could have a concussion, and the doctor will just want to make sure everything is okay. More often than not, it's just a precaution, but we don't want to risk it. I can't let you go home with someone who isn't a family member, so you're gonna have to work with me here."

Nodding, I held up the paper and pointed to the word 'mom'. The nurse, catching my drift, walked over to her computer to pull up my mom's contact information from my file and lifted her phone. I didn't want to bother my mother. Not that she's a bad mom or anything, but she's been...overwhelmed lately. This probably won't help.

Twenty minutes later, my mom burst into the nurse's office blubbering about her poor baby girl. She came straight to my side, talking so fast that I could only catch a word or two here and there, so I quickly signed that I was okay and that it was just a bump on the head. Ignoring me, she pressed a kiss on my forehead before turning to face the nurse so she could receive a full report on my health.

The second we got into the car, my mom launched into a full tirade about being terrified for my health, furious with the school board for not preventing bullying in the school, and telling me that we were going to press charges against Zach.

No, I signed to her. *He's in detention already, I don't want to make it worse.*

"He needs to be in *jail*, Ava," my mom replied. "You could have brain damage. We could sue."

I rolled my eyes, shaking my head, and turned away from her. It's one of my favorite parts about being deaf. I can end any conversation simply by looking away, and my parents knew it. They couldn't keep talking at me if I refused to look at their faces, and - without seeing them - they couldn't sign either. I love my mom, but I wasn't about to let her blow this thing out of proportion. That won't make Zach and his friends leave me alone, it'll just piss them off more.

After a few seconds, she started the car and we rumbled out of the parking lot to the hospital. I was glad to be getting out of school two hours early, but all of my joy was erased after we were stuck at the hospital for three and a half hours waiting to be seen and waiting for my test results. Everything came back normal, the doctor said, but I did have a mild concussion.

Upside? I got to skip the next day at school. Downside? My mom wouldn't leave me alone.

She used to be a nurse, but she quit after I was born. The doctor said I'd have no trouble living a normal life, even with my deafness, but she didn't want her baby to be 'unsupported' in the real world. My dad tried to convince her to go back to work, but then my little brother Evan was born. Evan is hearing, and - now 12 years old - he definitely didn't need my mom to stay home anymore than

I did, but she was struggling with the transition. Seventeen years as a stay-at-home mom makes it hard to break back into the working world, I guess.

Unfortunately, she really didn't have a choice. My dad's a Systems Engineer for the San Francisco Department of Public Health, and he's not in the picture anymore. It wasn't a huge deal - he was gone a lot when we were growing up since his job required him to regularly work nights and weekends - but it was a tough adjustment for my mom when he announced that he was moving out this summer. Somehow, he was letting us keep the house - and it was already paid off – otherwise, we'd be on the streets by now. I think it was his way of assuaging his guilt for abandoning his wife and two kids. He didn't put up a fuss about child support either, but even with his money, we were struggling to make ends meet.

It didn't help that we lived in one of the richest neighborhoods in San Francisco. Well, by 'in' the neighborhood, I mean a few blocks away, but still. We've lived here my entire life, but thanks to the tech boom, we're gradually being edged out of our own neighborhood. If my mom didn't get a job soon, we'd probably have to leave the city.

I really didn't want that to happen. It's tough being the only deaf kid in your school, but this city made it worth it. So many things to see and do, and I could pretty much go anywhere without limitations. I couldn't imagine living in some small town without public transportation where, instead of being just another person in the crowd, I end up being some kind of freak.

Thankfully, I was graduating this year. As long as my mom could hold it together until then, I'd be fine. My school has some of the best academic programs in the city, and my grades were good enough that I should be able to get into the college of my choice. Luckily, money wasn't an option when it comes to college. I've been researching scholarship options for deaf students for the past two years, and I was fairly confident that I could pull it off.

Like I said, all we needed to do was make it through this year.

CHAPTER 5

By the time Evan got home from school, my mom was still ranting and raving about Zach and his friends.

"How could the school let them get away with this?" She asked me. "Maybe I should call their parents, I'm sure they'd be willing to do something."

No. They wouldn't. I know, because I've heard the stories about Zach's parents. They were rich ex-Silicon Valley executives who'd retired from 'real' jobs early to pursue side projects. For his dad, that apparently meant a speaking career and as many one-night stands he could muster, while Zach's mom focused on bringing her inner *Eat, Pray, Love* out thanks to yoga and extensive trips abroad.

They couldn't care less about their son. Not that I blame them because I couldn't care less about him either. Today, however, was unfortunate because today he just...well...he pissed me off. You know how some days you feel like you're teetering on the edge of doing something stupid for no good reason? That was me. Today. Except I went over the edge, and now my mom's on a rampage and the target Zach put on my back probably just grew tenfold.

Mom, please, I signed to her during a pause in her monologue about the evils of the school administration. *I graduate this year. I'm almost 18, and I'm going to college. It will all be over then, so can we let it die? Please?*

She stared back at me like I'd just grown a second head or said something in Chinese. I mean, technically - yes - I am speaking a second language, but it's been nearly two decades. I know she got my drift.

Standing abruptly, my mom exited the living room and went straight toward the kitchen. Toward a bottle of wine, if I wasn't mistaken. And I wasn't. A few seconds later she re-emerged gripping her trusty companion Will the Wineglass, as I named him, and stared at me while she gulped down the contents. Ever since my parents started fighting - even before my dad moved out - she always claimed that wine was simply something she enjoyed, a way to take the edge off. She didn't *need* it, she promised, but she liked it and it's 'heart-healthy'. And 'isn't it better for me to enjoy a glass or two of wine a night rather than smoke a pack a day?'

A glass or two turned into a bottle per night until her doctor prescribed her Xanax and warned about the potential dangers of combining it with alcohol. She backed off initially, but soon the Xanax wasn't enough. A glass once or twice a week wouldn't hurt, she told us a month after my dad left.

That was a year and a half ago. Now we're almost back to a bottle a night.

I escaped to my room the second my mom pulled out Will, and I silently apologized to Evan for leaving him alone with her tonight. Typically, I tried my best to shelter him from our mom's moods. I wanted him to have a normal childhood, normal teen years, so I painted mom as an eccentric - someone damaged yet completely lovable - but I knew he could see through the veil. She was a train wreck. A ticking bomb waiting to go off.

Luckily, she slept til noon most days - meaning she was sober enough by the time we got home from school to seem like your normal - loving parent, but I knew it was just a matter of time before that façade cracks too.

Hopefully, I can make it through college before that happens. I already feel guilty thinking about going across the country for school as it is. I don't want to leave Evan here alone, but Columbia University has always been my dream. I'll feel horrible if I go, sure, but what about if I stay? Evan and I have talked about it, and he wants me to go. He always tells me that I deserve a chance to find myself.

Funny how wise a twelve-year-old can be when he wants to be. (Keyword: wants.)

I'd already opened my computer and gotten halfway through an episode of Jessica Jones when my door cracked open. The light from the hallway distorted my screen, so I pushed myself off my stomach and faced the door to see my mom standing there. She didn't have Will with her, and she took a deep breath before crossing the room to perch on the side of my bed.

Reaching over my nightstand, she flicked on a lamp before turning to face me. I could smell the alcohol on her breath, sickly sweet with the tell-tale aroma of wine, and her eyes are rimmed with red from crying. She was still sniffling - I noticed the slight shake in her shoulders - when she grabbed my hands with both of hers and forced a half-smile.

"I've figured it out," she told me. "I know...I know you don't want me to talk to the school about that boy, and I won't. I promise. As long as he leaves you alone from now on, I'll let it go."

I lifted an eyebrow as if waiting for the second half of what she came in here to tell me.

"You're right. You are almost eighteen," she said. "That means you're legally an adult, so you can get cochlear implants without your dad's approval."

My hands flew out of hers as I scooted away from her, shaking my head furiously. No, no, a million times no. I never wanted cochlear implants, and I didn't want them now. We've had this conversation over and over again. While I don't agree with my dad's reasoning behind refusing to allow the procedure, I have to admit - I'm glad he did it. I don't want implants, and my mom knows this.

No, Mom, I told her. *I don't want them. I'm happy with the way I am now. I **like** being deaf.*

She shook her head, "Oh, sweetie. You don't know what you're saying..."

My hands immediately formed the words 'yes, I do' but she grabbed them before I could protest further.

"Ava," she said slowly, forming the words clearly to make sure I could understand. "The procedure is completely safe, I promise. I know it's scary to think about the surgery but think of the benefits. To be able to hear again! The whole world will be open to you."

Dropping one of my hands, she ran her left hand down the side of my face, "Just think about it, honey. You don't have to decide right now."

And with that, she left the room. I know I said she was a ticking time bomb, but damn. I didn't expect to be left sitting here with my world in shambles so soon.

Boom.

CHAPTER 6

I spent the next day at home binging on Netflix, grateful of the fact that my mom slept until one that day. I managed to finish the rest of Jessica Jones - and I mean, whoa, Kilgrave definitely gave me nightmares - before moving jumping back into season 3 of Friends. However, even Netflix couldn't save me from my mom's outbursts, so I was pretty anxious to get back to school on Thursday.

Most of the kids avoided me like the plague - which wasn't exactly different than normal - but now instead of pretending I didn't exist, they were staring at me as I walked down the hallway. Zach wasn't in my fourth period class, creative writing, so I'm assuming he's either in detention or he was suspended for a few days. Hopefully the latter, but I have my doubts. His family's wealthy, so the school probably doesn't want to risk pissing off rich parents.

I took my time in lunch, waiting until at least half the lunch period was over before I hurried into the cafeteria to buy an order of chili cheese fries and a carton of chocolate milk. It wasn't the healthiest of options, I know, but cheese fries are one of my guilty pleasures, so I couldn't pass it up. Plus, I've had a shitty week, so I think that's a decent excuse to skip the standard chicken patty and go straight for the good stuff.

Lunch lady Rebecca smiled at me, per usual, and I picked up my tray to locate an abandoned table at the side of the lunch room. A few minutes after sitting down, my eyes wander away from my computer screen and I nearly panic when I see Zach and his friends enter the lunchroom. Apparently, both of my theories were wrong, and he was probably just cutting class last period.

Suddenly, my half-eaten fries weren't as appetizing, and I quickly shut my laptop and slid it into my backpack. I wasn't planning on *avoiding* Zach forever, because screw that, but I certainly didn't want to hand him the opportunity to make my life hell. The asshole should at least have to work for it.

I turned my head back to my food, praying he wouldn't notice me, and - luckily enough - my prayers were answered. After a few seconds, I hazarded a glance to my right and saw Zach sitting at a table filled with the 'popular kids', which - at my school - meant the wealthier ones. His arm was draped over Lily McCallister, his on-again, off-again girlfriend, meaning they were probably back together. At least, they were for this week. Who knows about the next?

Crowded around the table with Zach and Lily were their friends - well, Lily's friends - Piper Rodriguez and Cora Patel. Piper's parents owned a slew of restaurants in New York City, San Francisco, and Los Angeles that were uber trendy, and Cora's older sister Riya was a model-turned-Instagram celebrity who hung out with the likes of Kendall Jenner and Gigi Hadid. Last I saw, she was invited to one of Taylor Swift's famous Fourth of July parties. Naturally, being two of the richest and most well-connected girls in school, they were also surrounded by their male counterparts, Andrew Everett and Jackson Quinn. Jackson and Piper had been dating pretty much since the 8th grade, and both boys were on the track team.

The last member of the table? Theo De Vries.

You know how most high schools have that 'one guy' who defies logic of what a popular guy should be? Theo was *that* guy. Not only was he the star of the track team, he was also second in our class, incredibly friendly, and - oh yeah - gorgeous. Like, male model gorgeous. It was unfair for any human being to look that good, let alone a high school student, but there he was sitting with his friends at the lunch table.

No idea how or why he put up with Zach because the thing that made Theo De Vries absolutely unbelievable? He actually seemed like a decent guy.

I haven't talked to him or anything (get it? Because I don't really 'talk'), but I have photography with him at the end of the day, and he's always respectful of our teacher, Mr. Buchanan, no matter how rowdy the class gets. Most people see photography as a blow-off class. I'm sure you're thinking, 'How hard can it be, right? Point and click.' That's basically the mindset of most of my classmates, but Theo was different. He actually *applied* himself, like he was interested in the subject and wanted to get better, and - considering photography's my favorite class...that gave him a one-up in my book.

He moved here with his family two years ago, when we were in tenth grade, so I barely knew him other than the few things I've observed in school and online. His Instagram account was mostly travel photos, and his parents both worked in the Valley. They were probably part of the reason he was pushing himself so hard in school - the guy was primed to get into the college of his choice - well, that and his athleticism. As a junior, he hit a new personal record in the 100m dash, demolishing the school's record, and placed third in the nation for high school students with a time of 10.1 seconds. If he keeps up his performance, the local paper said he's on track for an appearance at the next U.S. Olympic Team Trials.

Watching him now, however, I can't help but notice how different he seems from everything I've read about him. Not that I've done a lot of reading about him, obviously - because I'm not a creeper - but when you can't listen to the gossip around school about your classmates you have to do your own digging online to keep up. I try to follow everyone on social media - make sure that I'm tuned into the conversations - and it's pretty hard to miss news about Theo because he's basically the talk of the school.

You'd think he'd be cocky or talkative or anything, really, but that's the thing about Theo De Vries. He's not flirting with the girls, he's not pulling practical jokes with his friends, but his quiet smile could light up the dark side of the moon.

He glances at me, our eyes meeting briefly before I duck my head, and I can't help but think it.

I want to know more about Theo De Vries.

CHAPTER 7

By seventh period, my head was throbbing beneath my skull, and I could definitely use a cup of coffee. Or twelve. Apparently, the doctor told my mom that my concussion was mild - meaning I only got to skip one day of school - and she was supposed to call the school and inform them that I wasn't supposed to do much reading for the rest of the week, but she was passed out when I woke up this morning. I didn't feel like waking her, and now I suffered the consequences.

I walked to my desk at the front left corner of Mr. Buchanan's classroom and dropped my bag next to the seat before curling up in the chair. I was early, which was rare, so I lowered my forehead into my arms and rested my eyes for a minute before class began. This class was my haven - no real textbook, no boring lectures.

Mr. Buchanan believed in teaching through experience, so we were regularly assigned new projects that explored a different facet of film photography. Sometimes we focused on composition, other times on contrast, and sometimes the entire point of the project was to explore the world around us and discover something unique and beautiful where others might not see it. We even had a darkroom attached to the classroom, meaning we were probably one of the few high schools that still taught film photography, but I loved it. I was taking Photography II next semester, which focused on digital photography, but I wanted to start with film.

There's something so wonderful and tangible about it. No auto-settings to make the picture perfect for you. No computer to correct your mistakes. You have to know your camera, know the light, know your subject...to me, it made photography more intimate and so much more rewarding. I loved capturing a moment on film, developing it myself with the chemicals in the school's darkroom, and seeing the combination of talent and technical skill merge on that thin piece of photo paper.

This week's project was repetition, and our assignment was to find and photograph an example of natural repetition. We weren't allowed to touch or alter the subject (or subjects, in this case) at all, simply to observe and capture. I'd already taken my photos over the weekend and developed the roll of film on Monday, so I just needed to pick it up from where it hung to dry and select a photo to develop. We each turned in one finished image, so today would be spent in the darkroom choosing a shot, enlarging and focusing it, and making the print. Not all of my classmates were so diligent in their work - many chose to use their spare time to goof off or sleep - but I couldn't blame them.

Today, the temptation to be a slacker was very strong.

A touch on my shoulder brought me out of my thoughts, and I blinked a few times as I jerked upright. My head felt even more groggy than before - a mixture of my headache and sleepiness - and I wiped my face with my hands before turning around.

Theo De Vries looked back at me, a smile tugging up the corner of his lips. His mouth formed the word 'hey' and I stared back at him, feeling a little bit like a deer caught in headlights, before giving him a brief smile and a dorky wave.

Ugh. I waved. Instantly, I wanted to wither up and slink away, but instead, I kept my gaze leveled at him. I could tell my cheeks were burning pink, but - to be honest - there weren't a whole lot of options for me. What else was I supposed to do to say hello except to wave? At least I didn't sign hello, which is more like a salute, and I didn't feel like grabbing a piece of paper just to spell out 'hi'.

Somehow, he didn't seem to mind my stupidity and lifted up a tiny purple notebook. Worn at the edges, it took me a moment to recognize that it was *my* tiny purple notebook. The one I always carried with me, and the one I thought I lost after Zach knocked me down in the lunchroom.

The emotions running across my face must have been amusing - jumping from excitement to horror that Theo found it - because soon enough, he was laughing at me. I couldn't hear it, but I could see his shoulders shaking slightly from the movement, and his mouth turned up at the corners. I'm used to people laughing at me, but something about this was different. He didn't seem to be making fun of me, especially since his smile didn't quite reach his dark brown eyes, and no one around us seemed to be laughing with him.

"Here," Theo said, handing the purple notebook to me. "I thought you might want this back."

Stunned, I stare at him for a moment before signing, *Thank you.*

"I think that means thank you, so you're welcome," he replied. "And thank you, by the way. I really liked your drawing of Mrs. Santo. She makes a very convincing zombie."

My cheeks burned bright red again, and I smiled. Hesitating a moment, I flipped open the notebook and pulled a pencil out of my backpack before scribbling a note back to Theo.

You read it?

Sliding the notebook toward him, he takes it and nods, "I know I shouldn't have, but I was curious."

I grabbed the notebook and wrote back, *Curious? About the freaky deaf chick?*

"No," Theo told me. "Curious about the cute girl in my photography class."

Oh, I wrote to him, floored by his admission. *Thank you, then. I guess you were the one who helped me on Tuesday?*

His eyes glanced over my shoulder to the front of the classroom, and I followed them to discover that Mr. Buchanan was starting class. Giving Theo a quick grin, I flipped the notebook shut and spun around in my seat to face the front. We always started the class with a five to ten-minute lesson on some element of photography before diving into the real work, and today Mr. Buchanan was using the time to return last week's assignments with our grades.

Once he moved past our aisle, I felt another light tap on my shoulder and turned. Theo held up a small scrap of paper, clearly torn from the bottom of his notebook, and I took it from him.

Don't worry about Zach, his note said. *He's an asshole, but he should leave you alone now.*

Wrinkling my forehead, I turned back to look at Theo only to watch him stand and head toward the darkroom. He was flanked on either side by Cora and Andrew, both of them chatting away as they started their work, but he remained stoic. He looked lost in thought, like he was in his own little world - completely oblivious to his friends' conversation - until he turned to glance around the room. Looking away before our eyes met, I exhaled slowly and slipped his note back into my pocket and stood.

My project wasn't going to do itself, no matter how much I wanted it to, so I went through the rest of class like nothing had happened. Grabbing my film, I picked a frame I thought might work best and waited in the darkroom for an enlarger to become available. I could see Theo working quietly across the room, twisting the knob to focus his image, but an enlarger became available on the other side of the room and quickly claimed it.

There was no point in thinking about Theo De Vries and what his note meant because it didn't matter.

Right?

CHAPTER 8

The next day at school, I didn't see Theo all day. Sure, he could've been there. Maybe I was just missing him. But, in all honesty, it's kind of hard to miss him walking down the senior hallway at school when he practically parts the hallways like the Red Sea. When he wasn't at lunch, that's when I figured he had to have missed school today. (Because, as a high school student, lunch is everything.)

I didn't want to be disappointed. Really, I didn't.

How cliché is that? Girl meets boy. Girl is average (or below, depending on who you're asking), boy is not. Boy is nice to girl. Girl falls apart.

Swoon.

Vomit.

I never wanted to be that kind of girl, and - truthfully - I wasn't. Theo's allowed to miss school without me sending the search party, but...I don't know.

There was something about the way he was in class on Thursday that made me curious about him. Curious about the track all-star and genius that all of the girls loved but no one could catch. I mean, I didn't think I could catch him. I don't do 'catching'. Still, there's something about him - something beneath the surface - that I didn't notice before.

Curiosity killed the cat, and it might kill me too.

The school day went by blessedly fast, and - before I knew it - I was back in photography class. The seat behind me was empty, and it just bothered me. Theo was top of the class. He was a Grade A overachiever, which meant he never missed school. Ever.

Why wasn't he here? Was he sick? Was something wrong with his family? Was there an accident?

God, I really let the freight train run away with that one. I attempted to reel in my thoughts, focusing on the enlarged print I finished yesterday and filled out the sheet to turn the assignment into my teacher. We always self-graded our work, something that was difficult for some high school students (i.e. those who think they do no wrong and that the world revolves around them), but I liked it. It was an opportunity for introspection, a practice in looking for the flaws - looking beyond the surface and what you might normally see - to see what someone else might. To be the observer instead of the artist.

If you think about it, that's pretty rare in life. We create things - whether that's through our jobs, art, family, or whatever - and we rarely take a second look at them. A deeper look. When do we sit down to not only see but to understand the things that we often take for granted....what happens then? Something might pass by your notice every single day of your life, and until you force yourself to slow down and actually open your eyes...you might never truly *see* it.

I never wanted that to be me. I spent most of my life feeling invisible. No one could hear me, probably because I didn't actually speak out loud, but that never meant I didn't have things to say. When I got on the internet, that started to change. People listened to me. People understood me. They didn't mislabel me, shove me in a box marked "broken", and carry on with their lives like I didn't exist.

No, I've spent enough time being glanced over that I was determined not to be the kind of person who does the same thing. I wanted to see. I wanted to notice. I wanted to understand.

It probably helped that I can't hear. I mean, I'm definitely not Daredevil. I don't have superhuman vision or anything like that, but I do like to think that I notice things that others don't. When you have to rely on sight for so much - to communicate, to survive - then you start to realize that there's more to seeing than just keeping your eyes open.

When Theo wasn't in school on Friday, it made me wonder what exactly was beneath the surface there. Sure, no one has ever taken the time to find out what makes me tick. Why should I care about doing the same for someone else, let alone some guy that has barely spoken ten words to me?

I don't know.

Maybe part of me hopes there's more to Theo than meets the eye. Maybe I saw something, maybe I noticed something, that I just...haven't understood yet.

CHAPTER 9

By Saturday, I was itching to get out of the house and go somewhere besides school. I thought about getting a part-time job, something brainless to keep me occupied and give me some money, but I didn't want anything to interfere with my schoolwork. I mean, I get good grades already - I know that I'm decently smart - but, while my school tries to accommodate for me, they don't always succeed.

My teachers are supposed to face front when teaching, one of the few accommodations the school made for me, to allow me to read their lips, but they didn't always remember to do so. Not that I blamed them, of course, but what good is it to get the extra notes when the notes don't say, "Remember, this is going to be on the test."

Plus, I needed my free time for my sanity. I spent five days a week surrounded by idiots at school, then when I get home I'm forced to deal with my mom. I loved my mom, but it's a big ball of stress that I don't want to make any bigger. She decided to ramp up the guilt-factor too in the last few days since I got that stupid concussion, and instead of talking about cochlear implants once in a blue moon, she's been talking about them every damn day.

I left the house before my mom woke up, slipping a note under Evan's door to let him know where I was going, and headed to my favorite park. We lived in a wealthy area of San Francisco, just on the outskirts of the neighborhood, so it didn't take me long to arrive at Lake Merced Park.

Weekend walks through the park always made everything better. It was so peaceful and beautiful, wandering through trails, allowing my brain to relax so I could just exist. I spend all of my time on alert - watching, paying attention to everything - so it was nice to switch off. My mom hated it, told me it was dangerous to walk around by myself in a park where I couldn't hear anything, but after I saved up to buy myself a tiny stun gun and a rape whistle, she stopped fighting me on it.

Today, my stun gun remained tucked inside my crossbody bag as I walked the familiar paths through the park, allowing myself to soak up the sunshine and the greenery surrounding me. I had my camera slung around my neck, and I stopped every few seconds to take a picture of something new. Sometimes, living in a city means you forget what it's like to get lost away from cars and technology, but I loved walking by the lake where I could pretend I was somewhere else. In reality, I've only been outside of San Francisco a few times in my life.

I've been to Denver three times as a kid, back when my dad used to take us to visit his parents, but those visits stopped when my parents started fighting. Other than that, we did a family vacation once when I was six to Lake Tahoe to see the snow, but my mom basically had a nervous breakdown. She thought I was going to get lost or stolen or something - I don't really know, actually. All I know is my dad didn't want to put up with it again, so we haven't left the Bay Area since then.

Soon I crossed a bridge over the southern tip of the lake, heading up the road toward another jumble of trails sandwiched between the lake and the beach, before heading toward my favorite spot in the park.

Every weekend, I always ended up at the Observation Deck overlooking the ocean, staring out at the Pacific and watching the ant-like people on the beach below. I liked to take ten minutes to myself, even when surrounded by people, to stare at the water. The size and power of the ocean always left me in awe. I wanted to be like the ocean. Unafraid. Unbroken. Uncontrolled by mankind.

I got excited just thinking about, daydreams flitting through my head of all the things I want to do with my life. Moving to the East Coast. Working at an art gallery. Spending a life chasing beauty and capturing it with my camera. I didn't to possess it, like taking a souvenir for my collections, but I wanted to record it. I wanted to remember it - wild and untamed - for my own selfish reasons. No one could hear me speak, so I wanted my photos to do it for me. To scream at the world that I exist, that I'm watching, that I have things to say. Even if I couldn't hear, even if I didn't speak out loud - that didn't make me any less of a person. Call me crazy, but even I wanted to fit in somehow. Somewhere.

Sighing, I rested my forearms on the wooden railing at the edge of the Observation Deck. It wasn't as busy as some days, despite the perfect weather, and I loved the solitude. A gust of wind whipped around my face, tugging strands of blonde hair free from the confines of the braid running down the back of my head, and I smiled into it.

Lifting my camera, my green eyes wandered, turning away from the ocean and the people below, and I took a mental inventory of the Observation Deck. Two small children played in the middle, a woman in black yoga pants glancing up from her iPhone to check on them every few seconds, and a couple were heading back for the trails. A few other people leaned against the railing with me, including an older man who smiled at me when he noticed my camera, and a young man whose face I couldn't see.

I snapped a photo of him like that, staring out into the vast expanse of the ocean. He cut a lonely figure against the brilliant blue sky, and there was emotion etched into every curve of his body. This was a person who lived passionately, with every fiber of his being, and I found myself wishing to be like this stranger.

Then, the stranger moved, his warm brown eyes turning to connect with mine, and I gaped at the realization.

It's Theo.

CHAPTER 10

I lifted my hand a little, waving shyly at Theo, and I was surprised to see him return the gesture. His brown eyes looked dull, less warm than they had been on Thursday in class, and his facial features were drawn tight. I watched his jaw unclench as he offered me a hesitant smile - no more than one corner of his mouth curling upward - before he did the unexpected.

He came over to me.

"Hey," Theo said, glancing nervously at his feet.

I smiled back at him, unsure of how to proceed, while the awkwardness of the situation seeped through the air between us. I've visited this park almost every Saturday morning for the last two years, always ending with a trip to the Observation Deck, and I've never run into any of my classmates. I wasn't even sure I've run into my classmates anywhere in the last few years, so I'm not really sure how to handle myself in this situation. Normally people just smile and nod, giving me the polite brush-off, and that's only if they don't decide to ignore my existence entirely.

Shuffling my feet, I reached into the small yellow purse I carry with me and pulled out a tiny blue notebook with a stubby pencil. Being deaf, I try to be prepared for all circumstances. My yoga pants didn't have a pocket for the notebook I normally carried around, so I always kept a spare in my purse. Granted, I could just use my phone, but I didn't like risking it. What if the battery died? Plus, I was a sucker for the nostalgia.

What brings you here this early?

I scratched the note on the first blank page and handed it over to Theo. His smile broadened ever-so-slightly, but it still didn't reach his eyes as he reached for the pencil in my hand. My eyes grew wide as I jerked the notebook back to him, holding up a finger for him to wait, before jotting down a new message.

I can read lips, you know. If that's easier.

He chuckled, his shoulders shaking imperceptibly from the laughter I couldn't hear bubbling up from his chest.

"Needed to get out of the house," he tells me, his lips moving just slow enough that I can tell he's being considerate without being a dick like the people who exaggerate everything like I'm not only deaf but stupid. "You?"

Same, I scribbled on the paper. *Saturday morning tradition.*

His eyebrow lifted after he read the note, "Every week? Damn. This must be where you find your zen."

Shaking my head, I passed the notebook back to him.

I wish. It does keep me out of a padded cell, though, so that's a bonus.

"Sounds like I should join you," he replied. "This view sure beats therapy. Must make for some great photos."

Therapy? What would someone like Theo De Vries need therapy for? He's a track star, a shoo-in for salutatorian, his parents were loaded, *and* he's gorgeous. If life kept score, Theo would be at the top of the leaderboard without question.

It does, I wrote back to him. *It's the perfect escape from reality, even if it is only temporary.*

After passing the notebook back to me, he turned and looked out over the sandy beach far below us that stretched out to meet the ocean. Waves lapped against the surface, beating a pattern into the earth that I could see even if I couldn't feel it. It thrummed into my body every time I stepped into the ocean, the ceaseless rhythm tugging at me.

His eyes looked dark as he stared out at the endless expanse of blue. With his shoulders tensed as he leaned forward, I noticed that his fingers gripped the railing tightly. It almost seemed as if the water was tugging at him now - calling him away from here - and like he was barely holding on, like he wanted to answer. To disappear into its depths.

I lifted my camera to take a photo of him, unable to resist the urge, and Theo smiled as he turned back to face me, "So what did you come to escape from?"

I shrugged, rolling my eyes as I wrote three capital letters on the paper before flipping it around to show him.

"Mom," he repeated as he read it, nodding in agreement. "I get that."

I pointed at him, my green eyes filled with the question that I didn't think I needed to write down for him to understand. He sucked in a breath, grimacing as he leaned forward on the railing to glance back over the water.

The skin of his knuckles was pulled taut from the grip he held on the wood, and he released it after a few seconds before turning to face me with a small smile.

"Everything," he replied with a chuckle.

CHAPTER 11

When Theo said that, I felt like the air was sucked out of my lungs. I mean, here I was, overlooking the Pacific Ocean with the most popular and most attractive guy in school (not that I noticed or anything), and he just told me that he wants to escape from his life.

What do you do with that information? How do you respond?

And more importantly – what does that mean for me? I definitely don't have my shit together, not now and probably not any time soon, and Theo's someone with way more potential than I have.

I watched him carefully, waiting for him to crack a joke and point to a hidden camera tucked in the bushes, but nothing happens. Instead, he turned back to look out over the ocean and leaned forward on his arms. His jaw was tight, the muscles beneath his chiseled face rippling with tension, as I studied him carefully. Clearly, there was more to Theo than meets the eye, and I wasn't sure what to do about it.

Scribbling on the notepad, I held it out to him just as he turned and opened his mouth to speak.

"I'm sorry, I shouldn't ha--" he said, stopping to take the note from me.

Contrary to popular belief, I'm a good 'listener,' it said in hasty cursive.

He smiled, and - for the first time - it actually reached his eyes. I couldn't help but smile back at him, tucking a strand of loose hair behind my ear, while I watched his face carefully. I could see him deliberate, and I'm sure he weighed the pros and cons of telling me what was going on. We'd never had a conversation before, aside from Thursday, so the risks weren't huge for him.

Who was I going to tell?

Lifting his gaze to meet mine, I raised my hand flat to the center of my chest just below my neck and moved it in a clockwise motion a few times, signing to him out of habit. It was a simple gesture. As soon as I made it, I realized he probably had no idea what the hell I was saying, and I flushed pink.

Please, I wrote in the notebook, holding it up to him.

"Should we walk?" He asked, glancing around at the now-crowded Observation Deck. "Find someplace a bit more private?"

I nodded, beckoning him to follow me while I zipped my purse shut and popped the lens cap back on my camera. Keeping the pencil and notebook in one hand, in case I needed it during our walk, I glanced at Theo and gave him a reassuring smile while I lead him away from the people and back onto the trail.

It made me nervous, walking with him. I'm not really used to walking around with other people, except for

49

my family and other deaf people, and I was worried he'd try to start a conversation while I wasn't paying attention. It was easy for me to forget that people really enjoyed the 'walk and talk', because - for me - walking was so solitary. So peaceful.

Instead, I kept looking over at Theo every once in awhile to make sure he wasn't saying anything. I could always watch him while we walked, sure, but being deaf hasn't really helped my coordination that much. It's fairly common for people with hearing loss to have balance issues - at least 30% of deaf people fall into that boat with me, or so my doctor told me - and I really didn't want to increase the risk of a fall by taking my eyes off the path.

After a bit of walking, we came across some picnic tables off the side of the trail. The grass was overgrown around them, so much so that we couldn't really sit on the benches without being overwhelmed by it, but Theo still headed that way.

He turned to face me, offering up a hand, and said, "Sit on top?"

I smiled, accepting his help, and fought the urge to shiver when his warm hand closed around mine. He gripped my hand carefully, helping me keep my balance as I stepped up onto the bench before taking another step to the top of the table. Once I let go, his fingers trailing across my palm, I took a step toward the opposite side of the table and sat cross-legged on the top of it while he joined me.

Facing each other, I tucked my notebook and pencil between my legs before looking up at him. I wanted to do something, say something like 'go ahead', but I didn't want to rush him. So I waited, patiently, studying his face while he stared down at his hands.

"It's stupid," he finally spoke, lifting his eyes to meet mine. "I shouldn't even be telling you this."

I shook my head, shrugging my shoulders as if to say 'it's no big deal', before waiting for him to continue.

"There's just a lot of pressure on me right now," he admitted slowly. "Senior year. Track. Schoolwork. It's hard."

He hesitated, letting his gaze wander somewhere over my shoulder, before continuing, "There's so much noise. A lot of activity and none of it is what I want. But it doesn't matter what I want, not really, because my life is all about meeting expectations. It always has been. My parents, my coaches, my friends...they all want me to be this guy, this version of Theo, and it's getting to the point that..."

Exhaling slowly, he gave me a forced smile, "I've been wearing this mask for so long that it feels like I've forgotten who I really am."

We sat in silence for awhile, and I stared at the wood of the picnic table as I ran my fingers along the grain. When I invited him to talk to me, I don't know what I was thinking. That he'd have some superficial problem. A college girl broke up with him. His mom wanted him to do some charity event. I didn't expect this.

Picking off a flake of green paint from the weathered picnic table, I grabbed my notebook from where it rested between my legs and flipped it back open to a fresh page. Theo now had one knee pulled up against his chest, his arm hooked around it casually while he surveyed the surrounding area.

I wrote a new note to him, chewing on my lip as I thought of what to say, before tapping his arm to get his attention. He turned back to me, his eyes studying me thoughtfully in a way that made me want to slither out of my skin. I was used to being the watcher, not the watched, and I could feel the trail his eyes were burning on my skin as he accepted the notebook from me.

Who do you <u>want</u> to be?

Theo smiled, "That's the hitch, isn't it? I don't know. I wish I did, but...I guess I want to find out."

CHAPTER 12

After our talk, Theo walked with me to the north side of the park where he waited with me for my bus to come. We chatted a bit more, hardly more than superficial conversation, and when Bus 29 came into view, I told him goodbye and that I'd see him on Monday. It wasn't until I was almost at my stop that I realized I'd forgotten to ask him why he wasn't in school.

When Monday rolled around, I don't know, I think I expected things to go back to the way they were. Theo showed me a different side of himself in the park on Saturday, but that didn't necessarily *mean* anything, right? People can have a moment of weakness. Need a friend. Who knows? I was just in the right place at the right time.

The day went by slowly, and - for a Monday - it wasn't half bad. Shocker, I know. I saw Theo at lunch briefly. He walked in with Zach, Lily, and the others looking just as he had the week prior. It shouldn't be legal for someone that attractive to be a high school student, but there he was probably breaking hearts by simply breathing.

He spotted me and I smiled, like an idiot, but it was too late for me to take it back. I figured he'd ignore me. I was half expecting him to flip me the bird or something, even though I knew that wasn't his style, but he didn't. Instead, he smiled back at me. It was one of those small, secret smiles that you always imagine someone sending your way, and - even though he was across the cafeteria - I definitely got his message.

"Hey," he mouthed, just as Zach turned to catch the glance between us.

Oh god, of course, he did. The asshole stood there for a split second, saying something I couldn't make out to Theo, before smirking like an idiot and heading my way. Panic surged through me as I fought the urge to close my laptop and sprint out of the lunchroom, but instead, I straightened my shoulders and lifted my chin to face the oncoming storm.

It didn't come.

There I was being all brave and shit for nothing. Zach was intercepted halfway through his trek by Theo, who threw his arm around his shoulder and redirected him away from me. For the casual onlooker, they looked like two best friends chatting like always, but you have to remember that I am not the casual observer.

I noticed the way Zach's hands tightened into a fist, his jaw clenched as Theo pulled him away and whispered something to him, and he forced a sarcastic grin on his face as he responded. Once Theo dropped his arm, both of them dropped the act and I watched as Theo's carefree smile slipped for a split second as he glanced at me.

He rolled his eyes, and I couldn't help but smile.

I spent the rest of the day trying to decide whether or not I would talk to him, but by the time photography class rolled around I didn't have the courage. It was one of our few lecture days in class, and Mr. Buchanan already had the lights dimmed for the PowerPoint presentation. Because I couldn't see him very well in the dark, this meant I had a free pass to doodle on my notes as desired since he would give me a detailed set of notes after class.

I loved the photography, and he was one of the best teachers in the school when it came to accommodating for my hearing loss, but sometimes you just can't win. I learned to roll with it a while ago, and now my notebooks are filled with plenty of doodles.

Theo slid into the seat behind me, and I tapped my pen nervously against my desk while trying to decide what today's glorious artwork would be. Before I could decide, however, there was a poke on my shoulder. I twisted around to face Theo, barely able to make out the 'hey' he mouthed to me in the dark before I noticed the folded up sheet of paper he was passing to me.

Taking it, I turned back to the front and quietly unfolded the note to make out the words 'thank you' scratched on the very first line.

For what?

I scribbled back my reply, quickly folding the paper and passing it back to him. He took a few moments, and - without turning around - I wasn't sure if I should even expect a response. It's not like I could hear him writing or anything behind me, so I just kept my head down and stared at the blank notebook in front of me.

Another tap on my shoulder, and I retrieved the folded square of paper from Theo to reveal:

For listening. :)

A small smile tugged up the corners of my lips as I read his reference to my joke on Saturday. I hated it when people walked on eggshells around me. They treated me like I was invisible or like I was breakable, when - in reality - I was neither. I wanted to be normal. A normal teenage girl living a normal life in a normal city.

Mr. Buchanan took a step in my direction, and I quickly stashed the note under my notebook. This time, when I stared at the blank page in front of me, I wasn't thinking about photography class, what I was going to draw, or even the people who sucked in my school.

For once, just once, maybe not everyone sucked.

CHAPTER 13

The next few days at school was better than I could've expected. In a magic twist of events on Wednesday, Mr. Rutger had to leave less than ten minutes into class, so we spent the rest of the AP Bio watching a video under the not-so-watchful eye of the basketball coach. My next two classes were a blur, and - before I knew it - I was exiting the cafeteria with the rest of my schoolmates headed toward my fifth period class.

I took my sweet time in the hallway, partly to avoid the post-lunch rush and partly to delay the inevitable torture known as Calculus, and when I rounded the corner to my locker, I collided with another human being.

My hand flew up to my chest, forming a fist, and rotating in a clockwise motion for a few seconds - signing 'sorry' out of sheer instinct - while I looked up to see what kind of man-mountain I crashed into.

"Are you okay?" Theo asked, his brown eyes wide as he held me upright.

I nodded, adjusting my backpack over my shoulder and pushing a strand of blonde hair out of my face. It was lucky I ran into him instead of someone else like Zach, otherwise, I would've ended up on the ground for certain.

Instead, Theo took his time before letting go of my upper arms. He stepped back, increasing the distance between us to a more socially acceptable one, before giving me a half-hearted smile.

"Good," he said. "Sorry, I should've been paying more attention."

I shook my head. It's not his fault that I can't hear anyone coming around the corner. Normally, I know better than to walk close to the walls. It's a recipe for disaster, and I've been in more hallway collisions than I could possibly count, but today I was distracted.

Reaching for my back pocket, I started to pull out my tiny purple notebook to tell him otherwise, but he placed a hand on my arm to stop me. When I looked up at him, his brown eyes were dark as he frowned.

"I've got to go to class," he told me, dropping his hand and sidestepping me. "Sorry."

He was gone as fast as he appeared, and I was left standing next to the lockers like an idiot. At least two students crashed into my shoulder from behind, and I nearly lost my bag the second time, before I finally headed toward my locker to grab my Calculus textbook.

My encounter with Theo felt off.

Ugh, kill me now. I was becoming the girl I didn't want to be. The girl who *cared* about what a guy thought, a girl who was bothered that a guy like Theo was too busy to talk to her. I'd spent the greater part of my life doing just fine on my own, but an hour with Theo De Vries and it's like I'd thrown everything out the window.

Spinning on my heel, I hurried to my next class and plopped down at my desk with a sigh. I normally sat in the front of the room, but Mrs. Santo didn't require assigned seats so I opted for the back. A few of girls settled into seats next to me and continued their conversations as if my presence didn't matter.

Which it didn't. At least, not to them.

One of the girls even glanced at me, and I saw her lips form the words that I hated.

Poor Ava, she said to her friends when she thought I wasn't looking. One of them, known for being bitchier than most, smirked whilst meeting my gaze before adding, *What a freak.*

I bit my lip, preventing myself from doing something I knew I'd regret, and pulled out my phone instead. I didn't use Facebook, and Twitter was dedicated to my blog, so I used Instagram to keep tabs on everything going on in school. I followed Theo just like everyone else, so I opened up the app and typed in his username.

Pressing his latest photo, I pulled it up and scrolled through the comments.

Damn. Theo's senior picture made him look like a male model. Not that he needed any help in that department, but he definitely made the average high school male look insignificant by comparison. Sorry, guys.

There were tons of likes and comments on the photo, mostly girls sending him heart eyes emojis and kissy faces. There was even a debate between three girls - two of which who were sitting next to me at the moment - over whether or not Theo was the ultimate 'bae' in Lincoln High School, and someone suggested that the student body should put it up to a vote.

Gag me.

I know girls have to deal with this kind of shit all the time, but it's absolutely horrific to see it happening on someone's Instagram feed. I mean, it's not like these were random strangers. These were Theo's classmates for goodness sake, which meant he would have to face the people who made these comments on a regular basis.

If I were one of these girls, I wouldn't have the balls to do it. I can't even bring myself to leave a compliment on Sebastian Stan's Instagram, let alone someone I actually know because it just made me feel so awkward. Then again, I'm not the person receiving the compliments. It's gotta be different if you're used to the attention. Hell, it's probably second nature to guys like that to know how attractive they are, so why shouldn't people tell them?

I thumbed through a few more of Theo's Instagram photos, searching for...I don't know. Something. A reason for why he was the person he was. An glimpse into his personality. An explanation as to why the hell he was talking to me.

Online, his life seemed perfect. He was model gorgeous, 6'2", and incredibly smart. His family was loaded, he was the star of the track team, and his friends were the most popular kids in school. Everything about his Instagram feed screamed perfection. Most of the pictures were of other people, random things, and his dog. Even his *dog* looked perfect.

Plus, his Instagram didn't scream "look at me" like most people in our school. Out of his last thirty posts, there were only three photos of him. The first was his most recent post, sharing one of his senior pictures, while the second was a photo of him on vacation with Zach and Jackson.

His only selfie? Posted over a year ago.

Class started before I found anything useful, and I sighed as I tucked my phone back into my pocket and slung my backpack over my shoulder. Self-doubt was a bitch, yes, but I decided that I couldn't let that get me down.

Why worry about someone I barely knew? Still, I couldn't get over the pit in my stomach telling me that there was more to Theo than meets the eye. After our conversation at the park this weekend, I realized that he intrigued me.

What or why?

I didn't have a clue.

CHAPTER 14

The next day at school, I tried (read: failed) not to think about Theo. The evening before, I decided that he must have had some kind of family emergency that explained his behavior in the morning and his disappearance in the afternoon. It made sense, really. Maybe his grandma died or something, and he was upset about it. Understandably. Regardless, it was none of my business, and I wasn't about to ask him about it.

Instead, I distracted myself by tweeting jokes with some of my internet friends, relishing in the ability to be myself without reservation. The internet, with all its faults, was something of a blessing for me. While other people used it to hide behind a screen, allowing their worst selves to emerge, I found that it did the opposite. It was wonderful - liberating, even - and I appreciated the opportunity to connect with people all over the world.

The way I saw it? I couldn't be alone on this messed up planet.

With so many marginalized voices - from those were ignored to those who were too afraid to speak - I made it my mission to accept all of them. To embrace and accept the differences we all possess in a way that my own were rejected by the people around me.

It was a painful reminder of how isolated I was in reality at times, and my good mood soon slipped. After my third period AP Economics class ended, I grabbed my backpack and slung it over my shoulder to leave the classroom. The hallway was crowded with hordes of gossiping teenagers moving like a herd of cattle through the tiny space, so I took a deep breath before stepping into the masses.

A hand grabbed my elbow, tugging me backward and throwing me off-balance, so I tumbled to the side before I could right myself. In the blink of an eye, I prepared myself for the fall that never came. A warm arm was wrapped around my waist, and I took a deep breath before turning to face the owner of the arm.

"Hey," Theo said, smiling as my eyes grew wide in recognition.

Smiling back at him, I lifted my free hand and gave him a small wave of my hand to sign 'hello'.

"Sorry," he told me, speaking slow enough for me to read his lips without being obnoxious. "I didn't mean to scare you."

I raised an eyebrow, still holding my breath from the fact that his arm was still tightly wound around my waist, and pointed at my back pocket where my trusty purple notebook was stored. Theo picked up on my question of whether or not he had time to "chat", so I reached back and slid out the notebook along with a pen and smiled at him.

He moved his arm while I did so, slowly taking a step back so there was more of a normal distance between us, and I resisted the urge to take a step closer to him once more. His arm had been warm around my waist, his presence steadying, and - to be honest - I'd never been that close to a guy before, let alone a guy like Theo. Every bit of him invaded my senses, and I could still smell the hint of cologne lingering in the air between us.

Don't worry about it, I wrote on the notebook. *My balance is pretty terrible, so a three-year-old could easily knock me over.*

It's true. I'm not one of those cute and clumsy girls you read about in stories, like Bella in *Twilight* who would constantly trip over a twig on the floor and practically break her neck. In fact, I spend a lot of time doing yoga in my bedroom in an attempt to work on my coordination, but the sad fact of the matter is that my deafness has messed up my equilibrium enough that I can't help it. I hate it, but I couldn't help but notice that Theo seemed to think it was pretty funny.

"That bad, huh?" He replied with a smirk, the corner of his mouth tugging upward in a hidden smile.

I glared at him, and he raised his hands in defeat.

"Okay, okay," Theo said. He tucked his hands into his pockets, glancing at the floor before continuing, "I, um…"

Watching him carefully, I waited for his next words. When in conversation, I'd gotten pretty good about staying focused - you can't really let your mind wander until you hear someone talking when you can't hear.

Instead, I have to keep my eyes glued to their lips in case I miss something.

In that moment, I completely blanked. Something about staring at Theo De Vries lips completely threw me off in the most cliched way, and I didn't realize that he had spoken until his hand brushed mine sending a ripple of electricity up my arm.

"You okay?" He asked, his face marked with concern.

I nodded, inwardly slapping myself for being so stupid. Getting distracted by Theo's lips? One, c'mon. I wasn't that kind of girl, as I found myself repeating far too often these days. Two, even if I was, the chances of him being interested in me are slim to none. It's not that I'm horrible looking - I'm no model, but I think I look decent - but, in my experience, not many high school boys are interested in deaf girls.

Except assholes like Zach and his friends who want nothing but sex.

"I wanted to apologize for yesterday," he told me. "I didn't mean to brush you off, I just...I wasn't having the best day, and I let it get the best of me."

Was he apologizing for that? Really?

I was surprised that he would take the time to find me in the hallway to apologize for yesterday's encounter, but I couldn't help but be pleased that he did. After getting ignored by so many of my peers, it's kind of nice to have someone treat me like a human being again.

It's nothing, I scribbled on the paper, showing it to him.

The bell rang, or at least I assume it rang considering the number of students in the hallway just halved in the last five seconds. Theo sighed, his shoulders dropping at the sound, and I definitely felt the same way. I wasn't a fan of school, but I also wasn't a fan of being late to class.

Smiling at him, I pointed at my ear then to the ceiling indicating the bell, then I tucked my notebook back in my pocket. We always got a warning bell, meaning I had less than a minute to get to my creative writing class. I watched Theo for a second, both of us waiting for the other to do or say something to end the conversation, before nodding and taking a step backward to turn away from him.

His hand snaked out, grasping my wrist, and I turned back to face him. With his right hand, he raised his fist in front of his face - opening it up so his fingers flared out in the number five with his palm facing him - and moved it in a clockwise circle around his facial features before dropping it to his side.

Stunned, I stared at him for a split second as he smiled, released my wrist, and turned away from me to go to class.

Beautiful.

Theo De Vries just told me I was beautiful in sign language.

CHAPTER 15

By the time photography came around, my day was pretty much a big ball of blah. Lunch was abnormally gross, as they ran out of my favorite turkey wrap, and the other options were less than palatable. Rather than stomach mystery meat or a wilted salad, I snagged a protein bar from the snack bar in the corner and a bottle of apple juice. It probably wasn't enough to get me through the day, but I wasn't about to risk my stomach. If there's one thing I take seriously, it's my food.

I spent the next two periods after lunch trying not to overthink the fact that Theo learned fricking sign language to say something to me, let alone that the something was calling me 'beautiful'.

I mean, sure, he could've meant something else. Right? I thought to myself in calculus. *Probably not, because it's not like he called me a muffin when he meant to say blonde.*

Beautiful is applicable to a human being, so it wasn't like it was way off base. Not that I think I'm beautiful. I mean, I'm not bad looking, but beautiful? That's a little too narcissistic. I'm confident though. Ish.

Oh god, am I ugly?

Ugly and beautiful are two very different signs, so there's no way he meant ugly. I mean, am I even sure he was calling me beautiful? He could've been talking about...the weather.

Ava. I chide myself. *Stop freaking out over some boy.*

My life wasn't about to become one of those stories where the hottest guy in school falls for the total reject, because that shit's unrealistic and promotes false expectations, but then again I'm not a complete reject. I'm not a nerd, I'm not a loser, I'm just...I dunno. Nothing, really. I got hit on a lot by Zach and his friends, so I know they at least think I'm decent looking....or easy, but I refuse to think about that option.

It was just...surreal. I don't know. I'd spent so many years on my own, so many years learning to ignore the stares and the not-so-subtle comments (that, yes, I could understand), that it struck me as odd that he wanted to talk to me.

No one else did, so I guess I'd started to convince myself that it had less to do with them and more to do with me.

Maybe I was wrong. A part of me hoped I was wrong.

When I walked into photography class, I realized that Mr. Buchanan was absent - which was pretty rare, considering he was the kind of teacher who seemed like he actually *enjoyed* his job - and we had a substitute teacher. For photography, this meant the class was either spent as a study hall or watching a film because no substitute wanted to mess around with the chemicals used in class.

The classroom was pretty empty still, considering I tried to be early to all of my classes, so I plopped down on a desk on the opposite side of the room and pulled out a book. Sure, I could do my calculus homework, but who *wants* to do that? Besides, there was a reason I picked first period study hall. Good grades are important, yes, and I wanted to succeed, but there is a line and I draw it on the opposite side of calculus.

As my fellow students trickled in, I didn't pay attention when Theo took the seat behind me once more, and I was unfortunately scared shitless when the substitute abruptly shut off the lights and plunged the classroom into darkness.

Obviously, we're going with Option B. Movie day.

I sighed, tucking a bookmark into my well-loved copy of Shakespeare's *Much Ado About Nothing*, my favorite play that I'm re-reading for a report in Creative Writing, and shut the book. The substitute addressed the class, something I couldn't see because of the dim lighting, and promptly started the film. A few seconds in, I had to bite back a groan.

No subtitles.

If he was gonna shut off the lights and make it so I couldn't read, you'd think he'd at least give me *something* to do. It's not like I could whip out my laptop in the middle of the movie. I'd done that before with past substitutes, and I hated having to explain to them that I was deaf. It was an exercise in humiliation - for me, not them, unfortunately - because half the time they thought I was trying to pull a trick on them.

Shaking my head, I grabbed my notebook out of my backpack and flipped it open to a blank page. It was dark in the classroom - there weren't any windows in this or the adjoining darkroom intentionally - so I could hardly see the paper in front of me, but it was better than doing nothing. Sleep was always an option, but it made me nervous.

Would you really want to trust a bunch of teenagers to not do something terrible to you when you're unconscious? Especially if you couldn't hear them snickering around you? Didn't think so.

Something poked my shoulder, and I glanced at the person behind me to see the dim outline of Theo staring back at me. His eyes and teeth reflected the light of the projector at the front of the room, and I glanced down at his hand to see him holding a folded piece of paper up toward me.

I snagged it from him, biting back my smile, and faced the front before unfolding the note.

You're not missing much, Theo's scrawl said.

I smiled before writing back, *Good to know, but now I'm bored. :(*

Passing the note back to him, I tried not to look at him as he scribbled a response on the bottom of the paper. A few seconds later, there was another bump on my shoulder, so I took the note from him without turning around.

A tic-tac-toe board stared up at me, with the top left corner marked with an X. I couldn't hold back my smile anymore, and it took me a few seconds to snap out of my bliss before making a quick O for my move on the game before passing it back to him.

He passed it back, filling out another square with an X, and I noticed a fresh note written beside the tic-tac-toe board.

Loser pays for ice cream?

Blocking his three in a row, I wrote the word 'yes' next to his original note before passing it back to him. A few moves later, the paper brushed my shoulder and I opened it to see a big C drawn over the board - we tied - and another note written at the bottom.

Best out of three?

CHAPTER 16

He lost 13 times before he gave up.

I smiled as I unfolded the piece of paper that was now covered in our tic-tac-toe games, most of them marked with a large 'A' to show that I'd won the game, mixed with a handful of C's and a four measly T's.

This is embarrassing. I thought I was better at tic-tac-toe. My eleven-year-old self would be so disappointed.

I scribbled 'tsk tsk' in response, passing the note back to him, only to be surprised as the lights in the room flickered on without warning. Squinting until my eyes adjusted, I glanced around as my classmates began chatting with each other - signifying that the period wasn't over yet - and turned around to glance at Theo.

He turned the piece of paper my way so I could see his latest note.

Chocolate or vanilla?

Lifting an eyebrow, I took the pen from his hand and circled the word 'chocolate' twice. As if it was even an option. Vanilla was fine if it was covered in various toppings or mixed into a Dairy Queen Blizzard, but chocolate was my life's blood. I'm pretty sure I wouldn't have survived this long without it.

Theo nodded in approval, clearly I'd made the right choice, and he grabbed the pen from my hand. The moment his skin brushed mine, goose bumps spread up my arm, and I resisted the urge to shiver in response. Biting my lip, I stared at the desk in a failed attempt to hide the bright pink flush creeping into the apples of my cheeks.

I really needed to get out of the house more.

Tomorrow night?

My eyes grew wide. Friday night? Aka, one of the universally acknowledged 'date nights' in the language of every single teenager? That night?

Wait.

This wasn't a date, was it? If I was completely honest, I'd never been on a date before - the only people interested in me romantically were the type who liked to skip that part and go straight to the dirty deed, unfortunately - and I had no idea how to tell if that was what Theo was asking. My experience with the male gender was fairly limited, so I just stared at the paper for a few seconds before snapping out it.

I nodded slowly, watching as the corners of Theo's lips turned up in a hidden smile. It was slight - so small that anyone else might have missed it - but I couldn't help but be thrilled by the sight of it. His chocolate brown eyes met mine, and the breath caught in my chest. He'd caught me staring at him, drinking in the sight of his perfectly chiseled jaw that was covered with just the right amount of stubble, and my cheeks flamed red once more.

Theo slid the paper back to me, tapping it lightly to draw my attention to a fresh note scrawled across one of the only remaining blank portions.

I'll pick you up at 7?

***

By six forty-five on Friday evening, I was a nervous wreck. My mom was already on her second glass of wine while Evan had barricaded himself in his bedroom. Dad bought him a PlayStation for his birthday last month, and he'd grown more and more attached to it by the day. Part of me was convinced that I'd see a wire growing out of his head soon, connecting him to the game console permanently, but I knew that wasn't realistic.

After all, everything was wireless these days.

I'd spent about twenty-five minutes watching (and re-watching) a YouTube tutorial on how to curl your hair with a straightener, but after four attempts I gave up and twisted my blonde hair into a braid.

My hair was finally long enough for the braid to fall over one shoulder, the ends stopping just past my collarbone. I donated it two years ago to Locks of Love, opting for an edgy lob haircut that I hated, and it was finally long enough that it didn't drive me bonkers every day. No one enjoys the process of hair growing out and having that awful 'in-between' hairstyle.

Glancing at the clock, I realized I had less than five minutes before Theo said he'd pick me up. I hesitated before giving him my address at school yesterday, but I figured I could get out of the house before my mom got a chance to speak to him. Now, I was seriously regretting my decision.

I did a final check in the mirror, inspecting the simple liquid eyeliner I'd applied with a tiny flick of a cat eye, before shrugging. There wasn't any time to do anything else, whether it be a reapplication of mascara or wishing I'd looked up how to contour, so there was no point in fussing about it.

If Theo liked me, then he would like me - with or without flawless makeup - and I had no control over it. Even if I did, I had no desire to cake my face with so much product that it was unrecognizable. Shaping your eyebrows and enhancing your features was one thing, but drawing on a new face was another.

Do what you enjoy, I always believed. Love makeup? Like the transformations? Do it. Embrace it. Whatever makes you feel comfortable and confident.

Just...do it for yourself, not for someone else. You don't have to try to look or act or *be* a certain way to make someone like you, because - in the end - it isn't you they'll be liking. A carbon copy, a cheap imitation, sure, but not the real person beneath the mask.

I thought I'd spent my whole life without a mask, waiting for someone to notice and care about the person standing in front of them, but I was so comfortable in my bubble of complacency that I never realized the mask was my deafness. I let people believe that I was shy and quiet, never bothering to correct them because it was easier that way. It was safer than letting someone else in and getting burned over and over again.

My parents showed me the shitty side of humanity. Selfish and cruel, I was sure they didn't give a rat's ass about learning to communicate with their daughter. My mom was the epitome of a trust fund baby who'd fallen from grace, and she'd had her life handed to her on a silver spoon. Her accidental pregnancy with me, however, turned her fairytale life sour.

My grandparents disowned her, completely cutting her off, and my father's parents forced him to marry her. They resented me, both of them, if not for my disability then for my existence. I was the reminder of the lives they couldn't have, of the path they'd never take. For my mom, that drove her into a bottle. For my dad? He was so bitter that he'd been saddled with a wife and a defective kid that he'd slipped away year by year.

Sure, he put in his time. He played the doting father when I was an infant, not that I could remember, but when my grandmother passed unexpectedly it was like the curtain dropped to reveal the man beneath the mask.

After so many years I decided if they didn't care then why should anyone else? Who else would bother?

The doorbell rang - triggering a flashing light that went off in my bedroom to alert me - and pulled me out of my thoughts. The light was one of the few things my mom had convinced my dad to pay for when I was little when he failed to go out of his way to accommodate for my disability. He didn't want to coddle me, he claimed, so he scraped by with the bare minimum.

The bare minimum meaning I could answer the damn door when he was too lazy to do it himself. I grabbed my yellow purse, slinging it over my shoulder, before rushing out of my room and waving at my mom as I hurried through the house. She was polishing her glass of wine, only half aware that I was leaving, and I resisted the urge to roll my eyes as I made it to the front door.

Opening it, breathless, I smiled when I saw Theo standing on the other side.

"Ready to go?" He asked, motioning to the car idling in the street.

I nodded, reading his lips, and closed the door behind me. I was done hiding behind my mask, afraid to take a chance because I believed no one would take a chance on me, so I took a deep breath before smiling at Theo as he walked me to his car.

It was like I was standing at the edge of a cliff, watching the water swirl below me, and every muscle in my body was screaming at me to jump. Take a chance. Live your life. Let go of the fear and worry and inhibitions while you embrace the possibility that sometimes the risk is worth it.

I had a feeling I might be right.

CHAPTER 17

I'm not sure what I expected out of tonight, but Theo
definitely defied all expectations. And then some.

He escorted me to his car, opening and closing the
door for me like a true gentleman (even though the feminist
in me knew I could handle it myself), and drove us into
downtown. It was almost sunset, the light peeking between
buildings whilst failing to reach others. The hills of San
Francisco made chasing the sun a game, one I loved to play,
and I couldn't help but lift my iPhone to snap a photo of
Theo with the sunset burning a kaleidoscope of colors
behind him.

My hands brushed the rich leather interior of
Theo's car, noticing and appreciating the texture beneath
my fingertips. His car was far nicer than anything I'd ever
been in - an Audi, I think - and the black interiors were far
cleaner than I would've expected of any teenage boy's car.
A deep navy blue, it was immaculate both inside and out,
which only emphasized the fact that his family was
definitely wealthier than mine.

He found a parking spot on the street -
miraculously - and ducked out of the car to open the door
for me.

"Hungry?" He said as I watched his lips form the words.

My stomach rumbled, the vibration making me smile, and he smiled in time with me. I nodded, lifting the strap of my yellow purse and slinging it across my body, and flipped it open to grab my tiny notebook. Theo grabbed my hand, the warmth of his fingers against my own sending a spark of electricity through my body, and I looked up at him.

I've been practicing, he signed slowly, pointing first to his chest then making a fist with his right hand and running it along the length of his left pointer finger.

A smile erupted across my face whilst butterflies flitted in my stomach. I could feel my heartbeat racing, anticipation for the night building, and I bit my lip to keep myself from laughing out loud. It seemed so surreal that someone like Theo would learn sign language just for me - not only to give me a one-time compliment (which, let's admit it, any skeezeball could Google that for a pickup line) - but to actually *communicate* with me?

Part of me wanted to cry. My own parents hated using sign language to talk to me. My dad flat out refused to use it, and my mom only used it in certain circumstances. The only times I ever spoke in sign language to someone in a two-way conversation was with another deaf person at a meet-up. Both of my parents insisted upon me learning to read lips, saying that the only way I would be normal was if I could "act" normal by pretending to listen because no *normal* person would ever learn sign language to talk to me.

Normal. God, I hated that word.

It was my dad's favorite, spouting it around twenty-four seven like it was part of the Holy Trinity. Jesus, God, and the Holy Normal Ghost.

Gotta be normal, Ava. Can't have you being a weirdo. Need to act like a normal person, look like a normal person, pretend to be a normal person...because deaf certainly isn't normal.

My dad wanted me to mask my hearing impairment like it was something to be ashamed of, yet he refused to let my mom take me to get surgery for cochlear implants. Seems counterintuitive, right? But no. It's not *normal*. It's not normal for someone to mess with your brain. It's not normal to wear little devices on your ears that transmit signals directly to your brain.

He was so obsessed with that idea. The picket fence lifestyle with the happy little wife and two-point-five kids. He'd had plans to go far in life, even picked out the perfect little bride, but her accidental pregnancy threw a wrench in those plans. They knew my mom's parents were strict, but losing her trust fund? That was unforgivable, especially when I came along to make it even worse.

Funnily enough, Mom thought I needed the implants to be normal. I guess she figured it was better to have a daughter who could hear than one who pretended to fit in with everyone around her. Even now, four years after my dad refused to allow me to get the surgery, she still clung to it like it was some sort of cure-all.

Maybe she was right. Maybe I did need the implants. Maybe if I could hear, I'd be normal.

If only I could hear, I would be normal. If only I had the surgery, our lives would be better. If only I could hear, my mom wouldn't be an alcoholic.

I could imagine her saying all of these things - I'm sure she *has* said all of these things - and it's part of the reason it shook me to the core that Theo took the time to learn sign language for me. Sure, it's sweet regardless. It's a nice gesture. But the fact of the matter is that even my own *family* doesn't give a shit about learning sign language to talk to me. It was as if I had burdened them, forcing them to go out of their way to communicate with their own damn daughter, and here is this guy standing in front of me opting to speak in my language instead of his own.

And I had no idea why.

You okay? Theo signed, drawing me out of my thoughts.

I nodded, flashing him a brief smile, and tucked my notebook back in my purse. After looking unsure for a few moments, he gave me a thumbs up - laughing at himself in the process - and pointed down the street at a large black sign with the word "MAU" printed on it in red block letters.

Eat? He signed, bringing his fingers together and pointing them toward his mouth as if feeding himself a piece of bread.

Clutching my handbag to keep myself from shaking out of nervous excitement, I nodded before signing 'please' by running my flat hand in a clockwise circle above my chest.

Theo grinned. He held out his hand, the invitation striking me as yet another thing I couldn't have predicted about this evening and watched me patiently. His dark brown eyes seemed so full of emotion as they traced the lines of my face, my skin flushing red in the process, and I slowly reached out to place my hand in his.

Palm pressing against palm, our fingers laced together as he squeezed my hand gently and led me to the restaurant and out of my thoughts of normality.

After all, what is normal? Maybe this could be mine.

CHAPTER 18

"So, tell me about Ava," Theo said with a mischievous grin after we'd been shown to our table inside the Vietnamese restaurant.

MAU was fairly busy, a swarm of bodies crammed around tiny high-top tables with tall metal chairs. I'd never been here before, considering it was way more expensive than the little Vietnamese place close to our house, but I kinda liked the warm, dark interior. Theo held my hand as we wove through the tables after the host, and he stepped in front of her to pull out my seat for me before taking his own across the table.

I rolled my eyes at him, biting back a smile as I shook my head. We're in the middle of what I assume to be a loud restaurant, and he wants *me* to be the one doing the talking.

Funny.

I hid my smile behind the menu, pretending to be scanning through the massive assortment of noodles, but I didn't read a single word. Theo leaned forward on his elbows, and he used his right hand to hook a finger around my menu and tugged it away from my face.

"I'm serious, Ava," he told me, his eyes sparkling in the dim lighting. "I want to know more about you. I know you like taking pictures - that much is obvious - but tell me something new. Tell me a secret."

I shrugged before signing, *I don't have secrets.*

"No secrets?" He asked after a few seconds, probably guessing more than understanding my rapidly moving fingers, and I nodded. "I don't buy it."

The waitress interrupted him, a tiny brunette with tanned skin and a beaming smile, and I breathed a sigh of relief. I shared things with people behind a computer screen. On Twitter. Not face-to-face. Not to someone I saw at school every day. Not to someone like Theo.

I realized they were both staring at me, and I blushed - probably with that deer in the headlights look - as I looked up at Theo for help.

"Water to drink okay?" He asked, and I nodded at the waitress.

She left quickly, a disappointed look on her face, and I smacked myself in the face with the menu. Normally I did a great job of staying on top of my surroundings when I was out in public, making sure I paid attention to anything and everything that was going on so I didn't look like a moron, but I'd let the ball slip.

Thankfully, Theo managed to save me in a way that didn't make it obvious I was deaf.

Not that I was embarrassed about my deafness - the opposite, actually - but because I hated that stupid shocked look on people's faces when they scrambled to think about how to proceed. Do they shout? Do they mouth the words overdramatically? Do they even attempt to communicate with me or do they simply turn to whoever I'm with?

I could always see the options as they raced through their brains, and most wait staff tended to go with option three. Because deaf people can't communicate for themselves, right? Because deaf people are basically children. Helpless. Feeble. Broken.

Avoiding that was greatly appreciated.

Sorry, I signed to Theo after lowering the menu to the table.

He smiled, "For what?"

I'm bad at, I paused, unsure of how to continue. This? What is this?

"Ava," Theo placed his hand on top of mine, and a tingle ran up my arm from the contact. "Stop thinking so much. Just have fun with me, okay? I want you to have a good time."

I nodded, and Theo's grin stretched even further across his face causing my stomach to flip.

I am *so* in trouble.

CHAPTER 19

My date with Theo went better than I could've possibly imagined. I mean, sure, I had never been on a date before so the only things I had to base it off were Netflix and books, but it was still pretty spectacular. After we went to the Vietnamese restaurant, where Theo ordered for me without making me feel like I was a five-year-old, he tangled his fingers in mine and led me a few blocks over to Bi-Rite Creamery.

If you haven't been to San Francisco, you don't know what you're missing. And if you have? Well, you know what I'm talking about.

Already stuffed with Vietnamese, I still managed to find the room for Bi-Rite's "trifecta" which was a scoop of each: salted caramel, brown sugar with ginger caramel swirl, and malted vanilla with peanut brittle and chocolate. Theo ordered "Sam's Sundae," which was chocolate ice cream with blood orange olive oil, sea salt, and whipped cream - a combination that I discovered was surprising delicious after he let me sample it. Twice.

We took cheesy photos together, documenting the sticky sweetness of the ice cream coupled with beaming smiles as we enjoyed each other's company. I'd never felt so blissfully happy with someone, unburdened by the awareness of my disability and the need to compensate for it, and I loved the feeling. Even with my few deaf friends, the people I met at the deaf community group that met twice a month for social events, I still felt like I had to keep my guard up.

But with Theo?

I didn't have to pull out my handy-dandy notebook once. While Theo's sign language was elementary, at best, he knew how to fingerspell - which worked in a pinch - and, as long as I went slow, he could understand most of what I was saying without too much effort. He tried to sign along while he spoke, but I didn't have the heart to tell him I was focusing on his lips not his hands. Not when he was making this much of an effort to learn sign language for me.

Even when we sat in silence, it never felt awkward. Granted, I didn't exactly know what it was like to feel the need to fill the emptiness with sound, but I still felt self-conscious about sitting in silence with someone who was hearing. It made me feel...broken, like the only reason no one is talking is because they think I can't respond or communicate, and I could practically see their thoughts churning in their heads.

Poor Ava, if only she could hear.

My deafness was an impairment, sure, a disability to some, but it didn't make me inhuman. It didn't make me any less of a person, and it certainly didn't impact my brain function in any way, shape, or form.

I think that's what bothered me the most about people who treated me different because of my hearing loss. They have this idea that normal means you can hear the world around you, and if you can't then you're defective. You need to be fixed because you can't be whole, surely, without your hearing.

That's a load of bullshit, by the way.

There's no hard and fast set of rules defining normality, which is something I've learned more and more over the years. I thought I needed to be smarter, blonder, taller, skinnier - but none of it mattered if I couldn't hear. It's like I was branded with a blood red "D" on my chest.

Deaf.

Defective.

Different.

In reality, everyone has their own badge that sets them apart. We've all got one thing - or maybe more - that makes us unique, makes us abnormal, and that's not a bad thing. Whether or not you admit it, that's an entirely different story.

Theo didn't treat me like I was different like I was some fragile human being that needed to be handled with kid gloves, and that made me supremely happy. Around him, I felt like I could be myself. Every *part* of myself, including the deaf part.

He smiled at me as we wandered down the street, still eating our ice cream. Or rather, he was still eating his ice cream because mine had magically disappeared in 3.9 seconds flat. Content with taking in everything around me, I didn't even notice he was watching me carefully for a few seconds before I did a double take and flushed pink.

"What are you thinking?" He asked, waiting for me to pluck up enough courage to look at him so I could read his lips.

I lifted my iPhone, snapping a photo of him with a colorful mural painted on the brick wall behind him while the street light illuminated his features before I pointed to myself before flatting my hand and moving it in a circle toward myself, brushing against my chest twice to sign, *I'm happy.*

"Wait, I know what that means," Theo replied, skipping a few steps ahead so he could turn around and walk backward in front of me. "Um...you have indigestion?"

Shaking my head vigorously, I made a move to grab my notebook but he reached out to stop me. A broad smile on his face, he tugged my hand away from my handbag and pulled me so I kept walking.

"I think I can guess," he said, a mischievous gleam in his warm brown eyes. "You think I'm handsome. That's why you keep taking photos of me."

I shook my head, and Theo gripped his chest with one hand, feigning a bullet wound. Flushing, I bit my lip to keep myself from laughing.

"I'm wounded!" He stumbled backward, and I grabbed his elbow to pull him out of the way of an oncoming pedestrian. "Struck me, right here," he pointed at his heart. "The ego. I don't know if I can make it."

Giving him my best glare, Theo winked before dropping his hand and scooping another bite of ice cream into his mouth.

"What will you give me if I guess it correctly?"

His question struck me, and I struggled to keep my heart from racing out of my chest and up the street away from my body. Butterflies flipped in my stomach, and I chewed on my lip before signing, *I don't know.*

Theo grinned, "How about...you come to my track meet tomorrow and I'll collect my prize then?"

Watching him carefully, I waited a few seconds before nodding. He laughed, his shoulders shaking from it, and I beamed back at him. We'd come to a stop without me noticing, and Theo finished his ice cream and tossed it into a nearby trash can. Walking back to me, he fell into step beside me and bumped his shoulder against mine to draw my attention.

I'm happy too, he signed.

CHAPTER 20

Confession.

I'd never been to a track meet.

Truthfully, the only reason I'd ever been to an athletic event of any kind was that my little brother played soccer. However, with soccer, it was pretty easy to track what was going on without paying close attention. All I had to do was watch when they got close to a goal, really, and remember that my brother's team wore blue shirts.

Track was entirely different.

For starters, it got a little bit stressful sitting on the sidelines and waiting for an event to start. It's not like I could hear them firing the gun, so I had to keep my eyes peeled to make sure I didn't miss a single thing - especially because the shorter races were over so quickly!

The most important event for Theo was the 100-meter dash, according to the slew of newspaper articles I'd googled before heading to the meet because everyone was hoping he'd break his previous record - which was the school's record and third in the nation for high school students - of 10.1 seconds. I already knew he was expected to go to the next U.S. Olympic Team Trials, making this season the most important of his athletic career thus far.

It was exhilarating, watching him run because there was something so pure about it. Sure, other sports might seem more exciting to watch, but races were purely dependent on your body. Your feet, your muscles, your mind - pushing yourself to your very limits in the hopes that it will be good enough.

He dominated every event he participated in, and he even managed to shave off a few milliseconds from his personal record in the 100-meter dash. I could practically taste the excitement in the small crowd, everyone buzzing around me as they watched this kid from San Francisco push himself toward greatness. Personally, I think the other runners were even excited for him.

After the meet, I picked my way through the crowd to greet him. He was surrounded by his teammates, as well as several adults, so I hung back to avoid interrupting the group. Instead, I let my eyes wander and lifted my camera to take a few photos of the happy faces that surrounded me. Since I didn't know everyone here, I didn't want to draw any unnecessary attention to myself and put a damper on conversation. Funnily enough, being deaf does that. It's like some people think they have to stop talking around me, like they aren't sure how to be human anymore, when really I just want to blend in.

Theo, on the other hand, saw me instantly. He excused himself from the conversation, giving a polite smile to the couple standing next to him that I assumed were his parents, and narrowed the space between us in a few casual strides.

"Hi," he said with a timid smile. "What did you think?"

I grinned, giving him a thumbs up.

You're fast, I signed, unsure whether or not he knew what that meant.

"Does that mean fast?" He asked, earning a nod from me.

His smile broadened as he mimicked the sign, his hands forming two guns - with his index fingers pointing out - before pulling them up to the sky. I shook my head and grabbed his hands to bend his fingers as I directed his hands back toward his chest, almost as if pulling a trigger, before I realized that I'd eliminated the distance between us without hesitation. My cheeks flushed a bright pink, my eyes locked on where our hands met before I moved to drop his hands and take a step back.

Theo grabbed my hands, causing me to look up at his face, and brought my palm flat against his chest to move it in a clockwise circle along with his hand.

Please.

I stared at his hand on top of mine, the feeling of his heartbeat thrumming steadily beneath my palm, before meeting his gaze once more. His eyes were nearly unreadable as he stared down at me, and I realized in that moment that he was just as nervous as I was.

Nodding slowly, I watched as relief spread across Theo's features. He pulled my hand away from his chest, carefully tangling my fingers with his, and smiled at me.

"We're having a barbecue at my house," he said, dropping my other hand as he ran his hand across the back of his neck. "Will you come with me?"

I nodded again, and Theo grinned as he jerked his thumb at the crowd of people wandering toward the parking lot. The group of people he was talking to had already dispersed, and I recognized some of his friends as they climbed into various cars. Going to a barbecue at his house meant meeting more of his friends, and probably his parents, but honestly...I didn't care. With Theo holding my hand, I felt like I could take on the world.

We made our way to his car, stopping to grab a duffle bag that Theo had discarded earlier, and he opened the door to let me in the passenger's side first. Dumping his bag in the backseat, he circled the car and climbed in the driver's seat before starting the car. I could feel the engine coming to life, but the vibrations beneath me were more than I remembered the last time I was in his car, so I pushed my palm flat against the car door in surprise.

Theo jerked forward, twisting the knob on the radio in what I assumed to be the volume, before grinning sheepishly at me.

"Sorry," he said. "I like it loud."

I grabbed my cell phone from my pocket, opening the Notes app, and typed out a message to him before turning the screen so he could read it.

I could feel the music, the note said. *I liked it.*

He looked up at me questioningly, and I bit back a laugh as he realized I was telling the truth. I'd never ridden in a car with someone playing loud music, and I assumed most people either turned it down or off when I was in the vehicle with them. Feeling the vibrations coming through his car door was a new experience for me, and I definitely didn't mind it.

"Do you want me to turn it back up?" Theo asked.

I nodded, pressing one hand flat against the dashboard and leaning forward with the other to twist the same knob he'd used earlier to crank up the volume. He flinched, grabbing my hand and twisting it down a few notches, before laughing - probably at the stupid grin plastered across my face. I could feel the music pounding through the car, especially on the car door, and I liked feeling the rhythm beneath my fingertips.

Thank you, I signed to Theo with my left hand, keeping my right pressed flat against the door.

Theo smiled, the corners of his mouth tugging gently upward, and I was pleased to notice that it actually reached his eyes for once. I'm not sure if it was my silliness, the stupid grin on my face, or something else, but he actually seemed happy for once, which made my chest flood with warmth.

"You're welcome," he replied, and I knew he meant it.

CHAPTER 21

On Monday, I was surprised to find Theo waiting for me outside my locker after my creative writing class fourth period, and I smiled broadly at the sight of him. He was facing the other direction, staring off into the distance with a hazy look on his face, so I used the opportunity to sneak up behind him and cover his eyes with my hands.

When he whirled around to face me, a slight grin tugging up one corner of his mouth, I couldn't help but notice the lost expression still etched deep within his eyes. Even though he smiled, I could tell something was wrong - something he was trying to hide from me - and it made me frown.

You okay? I signed to him, depositing my books into my locker.

He nodded, waiting for me to shut the locker door and face him before responding, "Yeah. Just tired."

Your parents? I signed, remembering the stiff smiles on Mr. and Mrs. DeVries' faces when I met them at the barbecue this weekend.

After we had finished eating at the barbecue, Theo politely excused us from the post-track meet celebration so we could sneak into the house to be alone. His house was immaculately decorated, clearly the product of an interior designer and probably a housekeeper, but it wasn't as large as what I expected. Then again, living inside the city limits meant less square footage for the same astronomical price as a mansion, and his house was still twenty times nicer than my family's.

He told me about the pressure his parents put on him to follow in the family footsteps at Stanford, but all he wanted was to go to a smaller school out east.

"Less pressure," he had told me after the barbecue, wringing his hands together as he pushed aside the still-blank Stanford application forms resting on the kitchen counter. "Plus, Stanford is what *they* want. It's never been about me."

Apparently, arguments about Theo's future were frequent, and - as graduation grew closer - they only seemed to get worse. Remembering what he said at his house, I stared at him as he glanced over his shoulder at the school's hallway, almost as if worried that one of our classmates might rat him out to his parents.

"My dad wants to hire someone to fill out my Stanford application," Theo said, intertwining his fingers with mine as he led me down the hallway toward the cafeteria. "He's basically forcing my hand. I'll get in - I'm almost positive he'd bribe the school if there was a chance I wouldn't - and he's threatening to kick me out if I refuse to go."

I lifted my eyebrow, and Theo seemed to read my mind before I had to worry about signing a response.

"Crazy, I know," he muttered, turning the corner into the now-packed cafeteria.

We made our way through the student body, and I was surprised to discover him leading us toward his regular table. Piper Rodriguez and Jackson Everett, the school's shoe-in for prom king and queen, were already sitting down with Cora Patel and Theo's best friend Andrew. I bit my lip, nervously clinging to Theo's hand tighter than I intended to, but he gave me a reassuring squeeze before pulling out the chair for me to sit down.

"Chili cheese fries?" He asked, gesturing toward the dwindling food lines.

I nodded, flushing pink at the prospect of him getting my lunch in front of his friends, and he disappeared into the swarm of students. Exhaling slowly, I smiled awkwardly at the four people now staring directly at me.

"Hi," Cora said, offering me a little wave.

She seemed a little uncertain - well, they all did - but I was grateful that she at least made an effort. Then again, she was probably only doing it for Theo's sake.

"You can read lips, right?" Andrew asked, speaking a little slower than normal.

Theo probably told him about me, so I nodded and relief spread across everyone's features. The pressure began to dissipate instantly, with Piper and Jackson immediately returning to their conversation, as Cora turned to smile at me.

"That's so cool, how did you learn to read lips?" She asked, picking at the tray of food in front of her.

I shrugged, pulling out my notebook from my back pocket and scribbling the word 'practice' on it. She took it, smiling at the note, before letting Andrew see it. They both relaxed, and we fell into a comfortable flow of conversation between the three of us.

Surprisingly, both of them didn't seem to mind that I was deaf. It took some getting used to, especially since they had to wait for me to write a response that couldn't be answered by nodding yes or no, but I found a genuine smile creeping on my face by the time Theo returned to the table with two trays of chili cheese fries and two bottles of water.

"I like her," Andrew said to Theo, causing me to blush and stare down at my food.

Theo smiled, popping a french fry in his mouth before responding, "Me too."

His hand found mine beneath the table, our fingers twisting together as we ate, and I couldn't help but notice that this was the first time I'd eaten lunch with other people - and actually felt included - since elementary school. Back then, the teachers used to assign kids to sit with me, but everyone just ignored me. Little kids didn't know how to treat someone who was deaf, especially since they could hardly understand what 'deaf' actually meant, and I didn't hold it against them. Still, there was something really nice about feeling like I wasn't a freak for once in my life.

A tray plopped on the table, followed by a stack of books that vibrated the surface next to my right arm, and I jerked back to prevent my finger getting smashed beneath the pile. My heart rate skyrocketed, a side effect of having absolutely no warning that it was happening, and I turned to see Zach Kennedy smiling down at us.

"So this is a thing now, huh?" Zach said, falling into the seat next to me and helping himself to some of my fries.

I grimaced, wishing I could push the entire container into his face, but Theo's gentle squeeze on my hand kept me from doing so.

Barely.

Turning to face Theo, I barely caught the words 'drop it' before feeling Zach's arm loop around my shoulder. I shrugged him off, brushing against Theo in the process, and glared at the asshole ruining my lunch yet again.

"What's wrong?" Zach asked. "I'm just being friendly. I thought you wanted to make the freak feel like she belongs?"

Cora rolled her eyes, "Shut up, Zach. No one gives a shit about your opinion, so knock it off."

"I bet Ava cares," he snapped back, giving me a sleazy grin. "I bet she's willing to spread her legs for anyone these days, so I'm just putting my name in for Theo's sloppy seconds."

Theo's grip on my hand disappeared, as did his presence next to me, and - before I knew what was happening - Zach was sprawled on the floor with blood gushing from his nose. He scrambled to his feet, wiping the blood off with the back of his hand, and said something to Theo I couldn't quite make out before throwing a solid right hook that connected with Theo's jaw. The two of them locked together, exchanging blows while Jackson and Andrew scrambled to pull them apart, as several teachers rushed into the cafeteria to pull them apart and drag both boys down to the office.

Stunned, I grabbed my pen and scrawled a shaky note to Cora, who just shook her head at the message.

What the hell just happened?

CHAPTER 22

Theo wasn't in school the next day, but - luckily - neither was Zach. After the fight in the cafeteria, they both disappeared into the office leaving me to finish lunch at the table with Theo's friends.

Instead of talking, we all sat there without moving. I pushed my tray of fries forward, no longer hungry, as I recalled the look on Theo's face after he tackled Zach to the ground. He was the good kid - always even-tempered and relaxed, never the troublemaker - but he looked like he wanted to murder Zach. Even his friends seemed baffled like it somehow wasn't real. Theo didn't *do* fights, let alone beat the shit out of one of his friends.

I didn't hear from him that night either, even though I sent a text to see if he was okay, so I had to reassure myself that it probably meant nothing. He was just busy - or grounded - and I could talk to him about what happened in school.

By lunchtime, however, I realized he wasn't there. Two girls were talking about him in my AP Biology class, and I watched their lips carefully while they gossiped happily about the situation.

"Zach's dad is super pissed," girl number one said, Amber or Candace or whoever. "I heard Zach's in the hospital, so his dad is totally gonna sue."

Girl number two scoffed, "No way. Do you think Theo will get expelled? Maybe they'll send him to juvie - I could see him getting a few tattoos. That'd be hot."

"Yeah, right," girl number one replied. "I'm just wondering if they're gonna kick him off the track team or not. Sectionals are next month, and Coach would be *pissed* if Theo couldn't run."

A stab of guilt flooded through my chest at the thought that one fight - one stupid comment from Zach - had the potential to screw up Theo's future. Theo got into this whole mess because of me, which meant I couldn't help but feel guilty. And guilt, my friends, is a huge appetite killer.

When it was time for lunch, instead of heading to the line to get food, I swerved to the left to claim one of the empty tables in the corner so I could sit and stew in my thoughts. Less than a minute into my pity party, however, my solitude was shattered when a curvy brunette plopped dramatically into the seat next to me.

"Hey," Cora said, checking her phone with one hand while she took a bite of a cheese stick dipped in copious amounts of marinara.

I waved slightly, my eyes wide, as she smiled and gestured toward her tray.

"Mozz stick?" She asked, popping the rest of one into her mouth.

Shaking my head, she shrugged and opened her bottle of water to take a drink. While she did so, I grabbed my notebook from my bag, fishing for a pen so I could ask Cora Patel - one of the most popular girls in school - why the hell she was sitting with me. Before I could scratch a note down, however, two additional bodies appeared in the empty chairs around the table. Andrew grinned at me, saying hello, while Jackson reached across the table to grab on of Cora's cheese sticks.

"Have you talked to Theo yet?" Cora asked, turning to face me.

When I shook my head no, she frowned, "Bummer."

"It'll be all over by next week," Jackson shrugged. "Zach's being a dick, as usual, plus his parents are blowing it way out of proportion. He deserved way more than a broken nose. I just hope the school doesn't do something stupid."

A broken nose? Theo broke his nose? My eyes grew wide at the thought as Andrew opened his mouth to speak.

"I'm not really worried about the school," he told us while munching on some potato chips. "They're banking on big donations to the athletic program if Theo does well in the Olympic Trials. Everyone wants their kid to be the next Olympian, ya know? It's his parents I'm worried about."

My brain flipped into overdrive as I scribbled a response onto my notebook and held it up for them to read.

His parents? I wrote.

Andrew nodded, "His dad is, uh...notoriously strict."

"Yeah, but this is stupid," Cora interrupted. "It's not like it was Theo's fault. Zach started it. We were all there."

It's my fault, I wrote on my notebook, but Cora shook her head.

"Zach's an asshole," she stated. "Trust me, anything that happens has absolutely nothing to do with you."

Unconvinced, I stared down at the table until Cora nudged me with her elbow.

"Why don't you talk to Theo about it?" She asked. "I'm sure he'll tell you the same thing."

I shook my head, and she wrinkled her nose.

"Come on," she urged with a mischievous grin. "I'll drive you to his house after school. We're practically neighbors."

***

The rest of the day passed insanely fast, class after boring class blurring into each other as we were piled with more homework. By the time I packed my books into my already bulging backpack, Cora was already waiting for me by the front door of the school. She waved cheerfully, waiting for me to reach her, before hooking her arm with mine and steering me in the opposite direction of the bus stop. Half of the student body walked or used public transportation to get to school, but - considering our school had students from some of the wealthiest families in San Francisco - a surprising number of students drove.

Cora directed me to a shiny navy Prius before unlocking the doors as we both folded our legs into the vehicle. It only a year or two old, the interior spotless, and it was clearly fully loaded.

"My parents insist on me driving to school," Cora explained, waving her hand at the dashboard. "We live less than a mile from school, but they think it's 'dangerous' or some shit like that. I figured the least they could do was get me a car that's a little more green to make up for it, ya know?"

I smiled and nodded, surprised to discover that Cora was so down-to-earth. With a supermodel sister, I figured she would be just like most rich girls - snobby, entitled, and basically a walking cliché. With most of her friends driving BMWs, Audis, and other irrationally luxurious cars that no teenager should drive, I liked that Cora insisted on being practical and environmentally-friendly.

"Oh," she said, grabbing her phone and passing it to me before starting the car. "Can you put your number in my phone before I forget? I want an update after you leave Theo's tonight."

She wiggled her eyebrows suggestively, and I flushed pink as I smiled and shook my head. Her head tipped back as she laughed, and I felt the rest of the awkwardness between us slip away while she pulled out of the school parking lot. Cora was definitely not what I expected, and I think I was making my first friend at school.

After a few minutes of dodging traffic, we pulled up in front of Theo's house. Cora turned to face me, a knowing look on her face, and I passed her phone back to her whilst exhaling. Nervousness shot through me, especially as I remembered what happened yesterday, but Cora just smiled.

"Theo likes you, Ava," she reassured me, which definitely did the opposite of helping me calm down. "Go on! Go talk to him. Get out of my car, and I'll text you later."

She shooed me out the door, and I grinned as I climbed out of the passenger seat. Slinging my backpack over one shoulder, she waited for me to walk up to Theo's front door before waving at me and driving off, leaving me standing there like an absolute idiot while my heart slammed against my ribcage like a jackhammer.

The door opened before I could ring the doorbell - or run away - and panic surged through me. Theo's face appeared, a smile tugging up one corner of his mouth, while he swung the door open the rest of the way. His gray t-shirt clung perfectly to his chest, tight enough to display his athletic frame without being obnoxious, and I blushed when he caught my eyes trailing over his torso.

"Hey," he said with a smirk. "Cora just texted me, said she dropped you off."

Oh, of course she did. I was almost regretting this whole 'friend' thing.

Almost.

"Do you want to come in?" Theo asked, gesturing into the house.

Nodding, I adjusted my backpack on my shoulder as he stepped out of the way to let me in before closing the door. His living room was just as spotless as I remember, the only thing preventing it from looking like a magazine spread was the empty cereal bowl on the coffee table in front of the couch. There wasn't a TV in the living room, unlike most houses, and the walls were decorated with vivid abstract paintings instead. They offered the only splash of color in the otherwise monochromatic interior, along with a few potted plants sprinkled here and there, and I shifted uncomfortably while I waited for him to direct me from here.

"Upstairs?" Theo asked, and I nodded. I didn't want to stay in a room that perfect because I was afraid I would break something or leave a trail of dirt that would ruin the Instagram-worthy aesthetic.

After we climbed the stairs, he opened a door on the right, and we entered what appeared to be his bedroom. A massive window covered nearly an entire wall opposite the bed, while the other walls were painted a beautiful navy blue. Floating bookshelves decorated the wall above his desk, and nearly every surface of the dark brown furniture - looking straight out of a West Elm catalog - was covered in neat stacks of books.

A lamp illuminated the corner of the room with a warm glow, and I followed Theo into the room before he graciously took my bag and deposited it into his empty desk chair. He motioned for me to take a seat on the bed, which was covered with a simple white comforter that sported thin navy stripes. A mess of assorted pillows pushed against the headboard, and I resisted the urge to belly flop into them.

"So...how was school? My parents were pretty pissed, but it was worth it to see Zach knocked down a few pegs."

He sat down next to me on the bed. With a foot of space between us, my stomach twisted in nervous knots as I gave him an awkward thumbs up before sliding my notebook from my pocket.

Theo shook his head, "I, um…" he stared down at the floor sheepishly. "I was wondering if we could skip the notebook today."

My throat went dry. Did he not want to talk to me or something? My brain started scrambling for answers at a mile per minute before Theo flashed a small smile and pointed at the stack of books on his bedside table. I glanced over them, taking in the titles I failed to notice when I first walked into the room. *Beginner's ASL*, *Sign Language for Dummies*, *American Sign Language Dictionary*, and more stared back at me, and I turned back to Theo with wide eyes.

No school meant time to practice, he signed to me. *Can we try sign language only?*

Dumbfounded, I smiled at him before remembering to nod in response.

Of course, I signed. *You did this for me? You didn't have to.*

He hesitated, laughing nervously before saying, "Umm…say that again? Maybe a little slower? I'm not very good yet."

I repeated myself carefully, watching his face to make sure he was understanding every word.

Yes, he signed. *I wanted to make you smile.*

Unwittingly, I grinned - unable to bite it back - and he beamed at me.

Ava, he started to sign before stopping.

I watched him, waiting for his hands to form the next words in whatever he wanted to say, but - instead of moving to form words - one of his hands moved up to my face instead. Cupping my cheek gently, Theo leaned in slowly to eliminate the space between us until it was nonexistent, and my breath caught in my chest. His chocolate brown eyes flickered down to my lips - just for a split second - before his eyes locked with mine and his lips pressed against my own.

Rational thought flew out the window, as did any awareness of space or time, as our lips moved together. I'd never been kissed before, but instead of worrying about whether or not I was doing it right, I found myself following Theo's lead and getting lost in the sensation.

It was soft and sweet, perfectly imperfect, and nothing like the kisses I'd seen in the movies. Instead of fireworks erupting in my head, I felt warmth flooding through my entire body while butterflies flitted nervously in my stomach. Our noses smushed together, both of us breathlessly desperate for more of each other, as he brought his other hand to my waist and used his tongue to deepen the kiss.

Finally - impossibly - we broke apart. Oxygen flooded my lungs, the faint taste of vanilla lingering on my tongue. He smiled at me, our foreheads pressed together, as I blushed and bit my lip. While one hand kept its grip on my waist, almost as if he was nervous I might float away, he trailed his other hand down my arm until it rested on mine. He used his fingers to push mine flat before fingerspelling the word OK against my palm in a gesture that was both incredibly intimate yet sweet. Goose bumps covered my skin, and I nodded breathlessly.

That was definitely okay.

CHAPTER 23

The next morning, I found myself smiling before I even opened my eyes. Hanging out with Theo - kissing Theo - was completely unexpected, and it was by far one of the best things to happen to me in years. Butterflies still flitted around in my stomach at the thought of last night, of how we sat and talked for what seemed like ages before watching a movie. Theo switched on the subtitles for me without a second thought, and we curled up together on his bed like it was the most natural thing in the world.

I shivered at the memory of his arms around me, a smile ghosting at my lips as I recalled his warmth seeping through my clothes. The comforter on my bed couldn't even come close to keeping me as warm as that.

The light flickered in my bedroom, and I pushed myself upright to see my mom standing in the doorway. She was fully dressed, a rarity considering it was only 7:00 AM, and a thick layer of makeup was caked on her face to mask the dark circles that perpetually ringed her green eyes.

"Get up," she said, tossing a towel to me. "You've got a doctor's appointment at 8:30."

I do? I didn't know that. I checked the calendar hanging on our refrigerator door at least once every few days, and - while the basket full of kittens was adorable - it wasn't quite distracting enough to make me miss a doctor's appointment.

Since when? I signed, throwing back the covers. *What doctor?*

"Does it matter?" Mom asked, clearly annoyed. "Hurry up."

I rolled my eyes and sighed as my feet hit the floor. A morning doctor's appointment meant no school for at least half a day - something I normally wouldn't mind - but after last night with Theo, I needed the distraction only a mountain of homework could give. Crazy, I know. Grabbing my clothes from the closet, I wadded them up with my towel as I trudged to the bathroom and turned on the shower.

Something fishy was going on. As helpless as my mom was, she used the refrigerator calendar religiously. I think it was her way of coping with the guilt she felt about letting my brother and I practically raise ourselves. At least we were always on time! Plus, that didn't even begin to touch on the fact that she was awake well before noon, and - as far as I could tell - stone cold sober.

The hot water scalded my skin as I stepped into the shower, wincing as I twisted the handle to cool the stream ever-so-slightly, and I tried to let my muscles relax. I couldn't remember the last time my mom had accompanied me to a doctor's appointment, and the anticipation of the unexpected wasn't exactly doing great things for my rising stress levels.

I quickly finished my shower, stepping out and wrapping the towel around my body. Steam coated the mirror, so I used my hand to wipe some of it away and stared at my reflection. The blonde staring back at me sighed, her wet hair tangled into knots, as her green eyes narrowed. I didn't mind my appearance if I was completely honest. Sure, I'd had struggled with my self-esteem in the past. What teenage girl hasn't? Still, I was proud of the way I looked. I was proud of who I was - and that included my lack of hearing.

Truthfully, I actually enjoyed being deaf. As I tore my eyes away from my reflection and pulled on my clothes, I smiled as I realized that fact. Being deaf gave me armor. Like Bubble Boy, I was protected from the world in some strange way, but instead of feeling isolated I felt...special. How many people could experience the world the way I did?

***

What doctor are we seeing? I signed to my mom for the umpteenth time as we pulled into the parking garage near the UCSF Medical Center.

I'd been here countless times, to various buildings, so I knew the area relatively well. I bit my lip nervously as I unbuckled my seatbelt and climbed out of the car, frustrated that she'd ignored my question. Again.

We made our way to the street, my mother leading the way with quick, jerky steps, before crossing the street and heading toward a multistoried building. It seemed vaguely familiar - I knew I'd been here as a kid - but it wasn't until I read the words on the door that it struck me.

UCSF Head and Neck Surgery and Oncology.

Horror must've been etched on my face as I froze mid-step because my mom latched onto my arm and tugged me until we arrived at the reception area for the Douglas Grant Cochlear Implant Center.

What. The. Actual. Hell.

Mom, I signed frantically. *What the hell are we doing here? Please tell me this is some kind of joke.*

My mother frowned, "Watch your language. I'm sure several of the people here can understand what you're saying better than I can."

I don't give a flying fuck, I replied angrily, gritting my teeth as her face flushed pink. *Tell me why we're here.*

After almost ten minutes of awkward silence, a nurse stepped out into the waiting area, her warm brown eyes landing on me and my mother as she smiled.

"Ava Collins?" The nurse asked, completely unaware of the family drama she'd just interrupted.

My mother nodded, placing her hand on my back as she pushed me forward. She'd plastered a stupid fake grin on her face, the same one she gave to all of the repair guys that visited our house as she pretended not to be drunk and unemployed to make a good impression.

No, I signed angrily, jerking away so I could face her. *We're not doing this. I'm not doing this.*

"It's time, Ava," my mom replied, her face tinted a deep red as she glanced nervously at the waiting nurse. "We can talk about this later when we get home."

I shook my head, *I'm not going in there.*

"Don't be ridiculous," she snapped, looking more and more frazzled by the second. "You are seventeen years old and living under my roof, so you will do as I say and march your ass into that office. Do you understand me?"

I glared at her, my green eyes burning with the threat of angry tears, before brushing past her and giving her the middle finger on the way. A mother sitting with her young son looked shocked, her blue eyes going wide as she clapped her hand over her kid's eyes. The nurse's eyes were wide, but she slapped a rigid smile on her face as I followed her back to the examination room for the nightmare to begin.

CHAPTER 24

"So, Ava," a man in a white coat said to me, the skin around his blue eyes crinkling at the corners. "Are you okay with reading my lips or would you prefer sign language?"

I shrugged, earning a sharp glare from my mother, and the doctor's shoulders shook lightly as he chuckled.

"Okay then," he smiled broadly. "Basically, I wanted to go over the process of what we're going to be doing over the next few days and see if you have any questions before we begin."

Tightening my jaw, I looked away from him, my eyes trailing over the horrible artwork hanging on the walls instead of watching his mouth form words I didn't want to read. The tension in the room escalated at my obvious snub until it was almost palpable, and I could see my mom bristle out of the corner of my eye.

I hadn't done this since I was ten and got pissed at my mom for refusing to let me get a double scoop of ice cream at the beach one day. Livid, I'd spent the rest of the day ignoring her - okay, more like three hours - and refused to look at her for more than a split second. I even went so far as to squeeze my eyes shut when she tried to corner me.

Doing it now might be childish, much like it was then, but I was royally pissed. She could deal with it then, so she could deal with it now.

After several minutes of closely inspecting the painting of a vase of wild flowers and trying to decide whether it was real or a print, the doctor stood and placed a hand on my shoulder. I faced him, perturbed by the fact that he'd invaded my personal space *and* distracted me from my analysis, and frowned.

"Do you mind following me, Ava?" The doctor asked, his friendly blue eyes tearing down my resolve to be an asshole to him.

I nodded reluctantly, and he led me from the room whilst saying something indistinguishable to my mother as she carefully watched us leave. We were probably headed to do some stupid tests or something, things I'd already done before when I was a kid, and I frowned. My mom fidgeted in her seat as I passed her, probably wishing she had a bottle of wine to drown in, and I ignored the pleading look in her eyes as she mouthed the word 'behave' to me.

"Ava," the doctor said after turning to face me. We'd rounded the corner into the reception area, not a testing facility, and I lifted an eyebrow as he continued. "I need you to be honest with me. Can you do that?"

No, I wanted to say. I'm incapable of honesty, I'm a pathological liar who might murder you in a second.

Instead, I nodded.

"Do you want cochlear implants?" He asked, concern etched on his features. "This is a major surgery and since you'll be eighteen when you have the procedure done, I wanted to make sure you're in this 100%."

I stared at him, my eyes wide, and processed his words. It was almost as if he'd spoken Turkish - that's how shocked I was by what he'd said - and it took me a few seconds before I could compose myself enough to shake my head.

I don't want implants, I signed slowly, as he nodded in understanding. *My mom does. She thinks I need them.*

His lips form a tight-lipped smile, and his shoulders sag an inch as he sighs.

"Your mother loves you very much," he told me. "That much is obvious."

I clenched my fists to prevent myself from making a sarcastic remark, and he continued.

"Sometimes parents have a difficult time understanding where the child is coming from," he explained. "You'd be wrong if you thought you were the first kid dragged in here kicking and screaming."

The doctor grinned, and I smiled back at him for the first time. This certainly wasn't the conversation I expected to have with him, and I realized that I couldn't hate him even if I wanted to do so.

"Cochlear implants can be life-changing," he continued. "And, for most patients, they're a very *good* thing. Still, that doesn't mean they're right for everyone. It's a big decision, and it can be a terrifying one - especially when you're faced with losing part of your identity."

I nodded, thinking of my own hesitation which was nearly indistinguishable from the fear I felt about it.

"So, how about this," the doctor proposed. "I'm going to tell your mom that we don't really think you're a good candidate for the surgery at this time, that way you don't get any trouble at home from this decision."

My mouth dropped open, and he chuckled.

"There's a part two," he continued. "I want you to meet with an old patient of mine. No strings attached, no promises, nothing. Just have a cup of coffee with her and get to know the procedure and what it's like from someone who's been through it."

Hesitating for a moment, I nodded in agreement. I wanted to balk, but I knew he was right. Every decision should be fully-informed, especially one as big as this, instead of influenced by fear or emotion. Even if I never got implants, it wouldn't kill me to talk to someone who had.

Walking me back to the room where my mom was waiting, the doctor smiled warmly at me as he began to explain a slightly different version of the situation to my mom. Her face twisted in shock, followed by a combination of grief and anger before her jaw tightened.

"Thank you," I watched her say through gritted teeth, nodding at the doctor before leaving the room.

Signing a quick 'thank you' to him, I followed her to the exit and bit back a sigh of relief once we stepped outside into the sunshine. My mother's back was facing me, her shoulders hunched forward, and I took a few quick steps toward under until we were standing side-by-side. She glanced at me, her features unreadable, as she clutched her purse with a tight white-knuckle grip.

"Are you happy now, Ava?" She asked, turning in the middle of the sidewalk to face me. "Did you do that on purpose? Did you really have to embarrass me like that?"

What? I signed. *No. You heard the doctor. He said-*
-

"I know what he said," she snapped, her green eyes that looked so much like my own blazing with fury. "I'm asking if you decided to be a selfish little bitch on purpose or if you couldn't help yourself."

Staggering backward, her words hit me like a slap in the face. Anger contorted her face, the disgust she felt toward me evident, and I swallowed the lump in my throat as I stared back at her in shock.

"You can find your own way to school," she said, running a hand through her now-wild hair.

She hesitated a moment, her eyes flickering back to the building until she turned away from me to walk back to the parking garage. Standing there, unable to move or hardly even think, I watched as she disappeared, leaving me alone on the empty sidewalk.

CHAPTER 25

I don't know how, but I found myself standing outside of Theo's house instead of going to school like my mom said.

Okay, I know how - two buses and some walking until I ended up on a familiar street are how - but, after ringing the doorbell, I was standing there with some serious doubts as to *why* I ended up at Theo's house.

He opened the door, and we stared at each other for a split second before I flung my arms around his neck. Maybe our relationship or whatever this was didn't include random hugging, but - at that point - I didn't care. Instead of prying me off, Theo's arms wrapped around my waist as I stood on tiptoe to bury my face into his neck, the soft cotton of his t-shirt absorbing the traitor tears that escaped my eyes.

He held me like that for a few minutes at least, the two of us wrapped up together in the middle of his still-open doorway, before he pulled back a few inches. Releasing one hand, he used it to smooth back my hair, and I sniffled. My cheeks glowed pink as I noticed the dark tear stain on his navy shirt, and I moved to step away from him.

Theo refused to release his grip on my waist, however, so I tilted my head down to stare at our feet instead of meeting his curious brown eyes.

"Ava," he said after using his hand to gently tilt my chin back up. "What is it? What's wrong?"

I shrugged, shaking my head instead of signing anything, and Theo frowned. He steered me to the side, pushing the door shut, and dropped his hand from my waist only to tangle his fingers with my own. Pulling me upstairs, he didn't say another word until he pushed his bedroom door open. I took in the rumpled appearance of his bed and his clothing - a navy t-shirt with dark gray sweats - and instantly felt terrible.

I'd woken him up, like an idiot. After all, it was only 9:30 in the morning, and he didn't have to go to school this week. What teenager *wouldn't* be sleeping late in his situation?

I'm sorry, I signed, tugging my hand from his. *I didn't mean to wake you up. I can go.*

Theo shook his head, the corner of his mouth curling up in that minuscule smile I was coming to adore and grabbed my frantic hands before I could sign anything else.

"I didn't catch half of what you said after 'sorry'," he said, "but you're not leaving. Okay?"

Nodding, I sat next to him on the edge of his bed with our bodies angled toward each other. Theo didn't press me but sat silently while his warm eyes scoured my face for some sort of clue as to what was upsetting me. After a few moments, I pulled one of my hands from his to lift my purse from my shoulder and dropped it on the floor, kicking

122

off my shoes at the same time. Tucking my feet beneath me, I took a deep breath before meeting Theo's eyes once more.

My mom, I signed. *She's mad at me.*

He didn't say anything, his eyes moving between watching my face and my hands as I tried to explain in the simplest way possible.

She wants me to get cochlear implants, I told him, finger spelling the words 'cochlear implants' since I knew he probably wouldn't recognize the sign. *She wants to fix me, like being deaf is bad.*

Hesitating, I squeezed my eyes shut as I recalled her words to me on the street, and tears rolled down my cheeks.

Am I wrong? I asked him. *Is it selfish of me to not want the surgery?*

"You're not wrong," he reassured me. "Your mom just...she doesn't get it. And I'm sorry about that."

I don't think she'll ever get it, I reply bitterly. *She thinks I'm broken.*

Theo sighed, reaching up to wipe away yet another tear as it rolled down my face, and leaned forward to press a gentle kiss to my forehead. His lips are warm and featherlight against my skin, and the sweetness of the gesture pushed me over the edge until I was a sobbing mess in his arms. He held me close, pulling me flush against his body until we were laying back on the pillows. My head resting against his chest, he kept one arm tightly wrapped around my waist while the other brushed a strand of hair away from my tear-stained cheeks.

We stayed that way for what seems like an eternity, neither of us saying a word - spoken or signed - while I silently grieved. He didn't push me to talk more, to explain that it hurt all the more because I knew my father felt the same way, that I was a disappointment to my family, that the two people who were supposed to love and accept me no matter what both thought I needed to be fixed. My heart felt like it had shattered under the weight of it all, the years of repressed emotions and bitterness, of silently accepting my parents' behavior as something I deserved, all because of something that I couldn't change about myself. Now that I could and didn't want to do so, I felt like a colossal disappointment to my mother, like a freakish burden to my father, and I hated how much that broke my heart.

And so I cried. I cried out years of anguish until I had no more tears left, and Theo held me - his hand moving in slow rhythmic strokes across the bare skin of my arm - until I fell asleep, exhausted both mentally and physically.

I woke up when he shifted, pulling his arm out from beneath me, and I blushed.

Sorry, I signed before wiping my face, realizing that I'd probably made his arm fall asleep.

"It's okay," he said, repositioning himself with an extra pillow under his head. "I didn't mean to wake you."

I smiled sheepishly, *I didn't mean to do that.*

"What?" Theo asked. "Cry or fall asleep?"

Both, I replied.

He tucked a strand of hair behind my eyes, and goose bumps erupted on my skin.

"Don't worry about it," he reassured me. "It happens to all of us."

I lifted an eyebrow, *Even you?*

He nodded, and I was struck by his honesty. Theo was the only person who didn't treat me with kid gloves like I was some delicate china that could be broken at any time, and yet he made me feel incredibly special. It was the weirdest and best thing I'd ever experienced, and I found myself wanting to drown in the very essence of him.

"I have an idea," he said, and I chose to ignore the change of subject. "Do you want to go for a drive?"

Biting my lip, I nodded. Why not? Theo pushed himself upright, helping me to sit up as well, before swinging his long legs off the side of the bed. My eyes landed on the clock next to his bed while I ran a hand through my sleep-tangled hair, and I was surprised to see that it was already past eleven.

I pulled on my shoes, grabbing my purse, and followed Theo out to the street where his car was parked. He didn't bother changing, simply pocketed his phone and wallet, so I felt a little less self-conscious about my wrinkled t-shirt and swollen, red-rimmed eyes.

The car ride was quiet, neither of us talking, and we pulled into the parking lot of a large shopping mall south of the city. Instead of claiming a spot close to the building, Theo stayed toward the back where it was completely rid of both cars and people. Curious, I lifted an eyebrow as I turned to face him.

"I had this idea," he repeated, pulling out his phone and tapping the screen a few times to pull open an app I recognized but never used. "There are only a few things in this world that are actually *worth* hearing. You don't need to hear to talk - you can read lips, sign, write - and I don't

125

really think you need to hear to be able to listen to music either."

Tapping the screen of his phone once more, he reached forward and twisted the volume knob controlling the car's speakers. I could feel the vibration rocking my seat, and I gasped in surprise. It vibrated my bones in an upbeat rhythm, so much so that I found myself pressing my palm flat against the car door so I could feel it even more.

"Do you feel the bass?" Theo asked me, earning an enthusiastic nod from me as he mimed the action of playing guitar. "Good."

He cranked it further, the vibrations moving through every inch of my body that was in contact with the car, and I giggled excitedly before slapping a hand over my mouth. Theo's eyebrows lifted, shock and something I couldn't recognize etched on his features, as I stared at him in horror. He hesitated for a moment, but his features softened as he reached forward to grab my hand and pulled it away from my mouth.

"I...I've never heard you laugh before," he said slowly, his eyes soft as they ghosted over my features.

I chewed on my lip nervously, *I hate my laugh*.

My mind went back to elementary school, remembering all of the times I'd been teased for my odd-sounding laugh when I was a child. I couldn't hear it, so I didn't know if it sounded right or wrong, but - over the years - I'd taught myself to hide it no matter what. I couldn't actually remember the last time I'd laughed out loud.

Theo smiled, using his thumb to trace my bottom lip before pressing a soft kiss against my mouth. He pulled away, and my eyelids fluttered open just in time to see his chocolate eyes smiling down at me.

It's perfect, he signed. *Just like you.*

CHAPTER 26

The rest of the week flew by, something I was absolutely thrilled to have happened. I couldn't wait for Theo to come back to school, as stupid as that sounded.

Cora and I became friends almost overnight, and she even started picking me up from school in the morning to join her for a morning coffee run. It was weird yet awesome, and I appreciated her warm and talkative demeanor. She talked a *lot*, but she also made sure that she didn't drown me out. One night, she even asked me to teach her sign language and told me that she'd asked her parents to find her a tutor so she could go through a crash course.

"Let's face it," she texted me on Thursday night. "I'm never going to be fluent in French, but this is actually doable since I have you to practice with me. Plus, it'll look badass on my college applications."

I smiled, secretly pleased that she was going through so much effort, but I told her that she didn't need to do so much for me.

"Why not?" Cora replied. "You're my friend. This is what friends do."

Who could argue with that?

By Saturday, I was giddy with how the week had turned out. Between Theo and Cora, my senior year was shaping up to be radically better than I could've ever imagined, and I actually stopped counting the days until I could get out of that awful school and head to the East Coast for college. I wanted to go to Rhode Island School of Design, and I'd been dreaming about studying there since I was a kid. One of the best art schools in the world, I couldn't imagine anything more perfect than getting out of the house - escaping my parents - and throwing myself into my work.

Now? Now I didn't need the escape as much, and - as weird as that sounds - I was grateful. College was a big step, one I knew I was ready to take, but I was glad I got one last chance to enjoy life at home.

Theo texted me late the night before while I was binge-watching Supernatural on Netflix, and he invited me to meet him at the beach today to hang out. It wasn't warm enough for swimming, but the sun peeked through the clouds enough that I was excited about spending some time outdoors with Theo.

Dressed in my favorite shorts, sandals, and a burgundy cardigan over my t-shirt, I waved goodbye to my little brother before leaving the house and making my way to the beach. I recognized Theo's car in the parking lot after I got off the bus, and I quickly spotted him sitting on a large striped blanket.

Theo smiled when he saw me, warmth spreading over his features like the sun peeking over the horizon after a long moonless night, and the butterflies in my stomach kicked up a storm at the sight.

He waved in greeting before taking my hand after I kicked off my sandals to help me sit next to him on the blanket facing the ocean. The sun reflected off the water like a million glittering stars, and I squinted as I turned to face Theo.

Excited to go back to school this week? I signed, impressed that he seemed to understand each word.

He was learning quickly.

No, Theo replied in sign language, earning a beaming smile from me. *But that's whatever. I just need to get out of the house.*

I frowned, *Your dad?*

Theo nodded. His parents put a lot of pressure on him to succeed, and I knew his dad was pushing him more and more toward Stanford. The more he pushed, however, the more Theo balked. He knew his parents wanted what was best for him, but he also wanted to be able to make his own decisions about his life and future.

Did you send in your application to UNC? I asked, knowing it was one of his dream schools.

"Yeah..." Theo said, his words trailing from his lips as I watched them curl into a frown. "But what if I don't want to go to college right away?"

I shrugged, *Why not? Take a year off? Travel? Focus on the Olympics.*

"Maybe," Theo murmured. "Maybe."

He fell silent, and I suddenly felt horrible. I'd reminded him about the upcoming Olympic Trials, another monumental source of stress that I knew he'd come to resent. At eighteen, Theo should be focused on enjoying the rest of his time in high school, preparing for his future - on his own terms - instead of facing this much pressure. I couldn't imagine how he dealt with all of it and managed to keep a smile on his face.

We sat for a moment, neither of us speaking, and Theo turned away from me to scan the horizon. I lifted my hands to apologize, but without him facing me I knew it would be useless. I waited a moment, my heart racing with anticipation of what I was considering, before taking a deep breath.

"Theo," I said, my mouth forming the word I'd been practicing in my mirror all week.

I had no idea if any sound came out, or - if it did - if I said his name correctly. So much of learning speech is audible, connecting the dots between what you're seeing and mimicking it, and I hated talking because I knew I couldn't do that. Plus, I couldn't see exactly how people used their tongue to hit the back of their front teeth to form the 'th' sound, so I had to guess for myself. I'd watched countless YouTube videos and read pronunciation guides, but I knew my speech would probably still sound off. I hadn't used my voice in front of another human being in over a decade, and there I was sitting on the beach wondering if he'd heard me, if he'd turn around to face me, how he'd react.

He did turn to face me, slowly, his eyes filled with both confusion and wonder.

"Say it again," Theo told me, his eyes glued to my face.

I flushed pink and shook my head, mortified, but Theo grabbed my hand with his and held it tight.

"Please?" He asked, his brown eyes pleading. "I just...I've never heard your voice before."

I licked my lips, glancing at our intertwined fingers for a split second before I looked up at him and spoke.

"Theo," I said again, taking in every minute change in his facial expressions at the sound of my voice. The corner of his mouth turned up in a smile as he squeezed my hand, and I decided to continue. To say the other three words I'd been practicing.

"I like you."

He eliminated the distance between us in an instant, pressing his lips against mine in a gentle kiss, before pulling back and resting his forehead against my own.

"I like you too," he told me. "And I love the sound of your voice."

CHAPTER 27

Sunday passed quickly, and I woke up an hour before my alarm on Monday morning even though I'd stayed up late texting Cora.

She was obsessing over whether or not I thought Theo would ask me to the prom, which - given the fact that I never intended to go to prom in the first place - I wasn't really bothered either way. I mean, yes, it would be nice for him to ask me. More than nice, really. But we weren't even dating, not officially, so I didn't want to expect anything from him.

Cora, for the record, disagreed. She was under the impression that we were very much "official" given the fact that he'd gotten into a fight and was even suspended for me.

"That doesn't exactly scream casual," she texted me last night, followed by a billion or so winking emojis.

I grinned at the memory and rushed through getting ready. A quick shower, braiding my hair, and suddenly I was sitting at the kitchen counter with a half-eaten bowl of Cap'n Crunch and an hour left before Cora was supposed to pick me up for school.

Instead of waiting for her, I grabbed one of the travel mugs from the cabinet and filled it with coffee before texting Cora that I was going to walk to school instead. I had some extra energy to burn, and a brisk walk coupled with an early morning study session in the library would probably be good for both me and my grades.

Practically skipping to school, the librarian smiled at me from where she stacked books on a cart to be reshelved, and I headed toward a small table in the back so I could study for my upcoming calculus exam. Mrs. Santo's tests were notoriously difficult, and I'd barely scraped by with a B on the last one. It was a good grade, especially considering the subject, but I'd studied for at least twelve hours the week before that test, and thus far I'd racked up a grand total of zero study hours for this unit.

I quickly lost track of time, and - before I knew it - the librarian was tapping my shoulder to point at the clock.

Shit.

First period started five minutes ago, and I needed to pee before running to study hall across the school.

Stuffing my textbook and notes in my bag, I slung my backpack over my shoulder as I gave the librarian a friendly smile. Her usually cheery face was stoic, her thin lips pressed into a grim line, but I ignored the urge to roll my eyes as I rushed out of the library. She probably frowned upon tardiness.

A surprising number of students were still in the hallways, most of them clustered in groups around an open locker. They all turned inward, most with their backs to me, so I couldn't see what any of them were saying.

Jackson, one of Theo's teammates in track, rounded the corner in front of me, and I lifted my hand to wave as I adjusted my backpack, but his eyes stayed glued to the floor. Instead of waiting to catch his attention, I turned the corner and crossed the hallway to duck into the girl's bathroom. Another group of girls huddled in the corner, and I noticed that several of them had red, puffy eyes as I ducked into the first empty stall.

They'd disappeared by the time I finished, so I shrugged as I heaved my backpack over my shoulder once more as I washed my hands. The water scalded my skin as I scrubbed my hands, drying them on a paper towel before tossing it into the trash and rushing out of the bathroom.

I nearly collided with another girl, a brunette I recognized from my creative writing class, and she stared at me with wide eyes before I sidestepped her and headed back into the hallway.

Luckily, they don't really give detentions for being stupid late for study hall because I definitely didn't want to stay after school when I hadn't even missed part of a lesson. Pretty sure most of the study hall advisors knew that losing some of your time to frantically finish last night's homework is punishment enough.

When I passed the main office, I noticed an oddly large number of students clustered by the front desk. Several of the school's guidance counselors were in there too, along with a few adults I didn't recognize, and half of them turned to stare at me as I walked past.

A hand wrapped around my elbow, tugging me gently to turn around, and I was surprised to see Cora staring at me. Her brown eyes, normally accentuated with

immaculate eyeliner, were bare and bloodshot, and tear
stains tracked down both of her cheeks. Her hair was pulled
into a messy bun on top of her head, something I'd never
seen her do before, and she was wearing a slouchy
sweatshirt over her leggings.

Are you okay? I signed, concerned by her grief-
stricken appearance.

She shook her head, opening and closing her mouth
without forming any words. Another tear rolled down her
cheek, and I adjusted my backpack on my shoulder.

What? I asked her. *What is it?*

That's when I noticed everyone staring at me. The
entire hallway - and everyone in the office - watched the
two of us as Cora took a deep breath. My eyes flickered
back to her face as she said the words.

Slowly.

Carefully.

Painfully.

CHAPTER 28

I don't really remember what happened next because it was so much of a blur. I couldn't get more than a few words out of Cora before I took off, confused and frustrated, and headed for the school's front doors.

Nobody stopped me, and I wasn't sure if that was because I looked like I was on the warpath or on the verge of breaking. Truthfully, I couldn't tell you which it was then. I still couldn't to this day.

Instead, I ended up walking just over a mile in the late morning sun through San Francisco, veering in the opposite direction of my house. I couldn't go home. Not when every cell in my body was screaming at me, every bone aching, as I threatened to crumble and break on the sidewalk beneath the cloudless pale blue sky.

I just needed to talk to Theo, I repeated over and over to myself, hardly even realizing that my feet had already brought me to the street in front of his house. The street was lined with cars, all of them parallel parked down the busy street. I exhaled at the sight of his house, letting in what felt like my first breath of fresh air since I left school, as I walked up to his front door.

My knuckles rapped heavily against the wood, knocking instead of ringing the doorbell, and I waited a few seconds before knocking again. Another trio of impatient knocks and I could feel my skin already bruising from the rough contact. I lifted my hand to knock again, but the door swung open slowly before I could make contact.

Theo's mom stood across from me, her eyebrows knit together in confusion as she stared back at me. The way she looked at me burned while I signed frantically, forgetting for a moment that she couldn't understand a word I was saying.

Where is Theo? I asked, gritting my teeth as I struggled to maintain my composure in front of the woman I knew disapproved of me.

I shifted uncomfortably, running a hand under my eye to brush away the single rogue tear that managed to escape from the corner of my eye. I wouldn't cry. Not yet. Not here. Not in front of her.

"Theo," I finally said, forcing the word through my lips as emotion flitted across her features. "Where is Theo?"

Her jaw tightened, and I saw something in her eyes - a crack in her composure - that unsettled me.

Dropping my bag on the front step, I pushed past her. I couldn't stand there for another second, not when my head felt like it might spontaneously combust at any second. I ran through the living room without stopping, ignoring the crowd of well-dressed people who stared at my unconventional entrance.

I didn't care. I just needed to know.

Taking the stairs two at a time, I crashed into Theo's room in a breathless frenzy. My eyes raked over the familiar sight - the stack of sign language books on his bedside table, the screensaver of his iMac displaying the time, the soft yellow light of his lamp illuminating the far corner. His bed was immaculately made, the comforter tucked under the mattress with precision, and the mountain of pillows was actually organized for once. Everything was in perfect order, everything in the same place as it was the last time I was here, everything but one thing.

CHAPTER 29

It's been five years.

Five years, almost to the day, and I found myself sitting in the back of the mall parking lot where Theo brought me to "feel" the music through his car speakers on an afternoon so long ago. He'd given me a mix CD a few days later, insisting that - if I was going to own a CD - it should at least be filled with good music.

The irony of it still brought a smile to my face. A deaf girl getting a mixtape. I kept it, all these years, still tucked in the protective white paper sleeve with my name scribbled across the front in that familiar black Sharpie.

I gripped the steering wheel tightly, my knuckles turning white as I stared blankly through the windshield. I'd taken driver's training a year into college, thanks to Cora's insistence, and I got my license even though I still preferred to walk everywhere. Cora joked that it was her summer project after our freshman year of college.

Surprisingly enough, Cora and I went to neighboring schools on the East Coast. I went to RISD, which happened to be on the same campus as Brown University where she was accepted. We went together like peanut butter and jelly, never straying too far from the other, and eventually, we even got an apartment together in a nice neighborhood near downtown Boston. She graduated with a degree in public relations, and she didn't even need her sister's status as a supermodel definitely to land an awesome job with a glitzy firm in the city.

I found myself majoring in photography. It was the only thing I wanted to do with my life these days, hide behind the lens of a camera and capture fleeting moments before they slipped through my fingers, and I'd discovered a talent for looking at the world with my own unique perspective.

My professors wondered if it had something to do with my lack of hearing, if the deprivation of one sense made it easier for me to see the beauty in the world around me, and I guess they were right in a way. I considered myself lucky for having that skill. Perspective, after all, is the great differentiator. Sometimes the line isn't so blurred between good or bad. Right or wrong. Broken or beautiful.

Sometimes I couldn't help but think that my photographs were just a mask, a way to fill my life up so no one would notice how empty I'd become. I could feel myself bleed in black and white, every click of the shutter vibrating through my bones like a silent and deadly trigger.

I sucked in a breath, pushing my thoughts back to the present, and glanced over at the passenger seat. A familiar object stared up at me, its edges bent and worn from five years of neglect, and I slowly relinquished my grip on the steering wheel to brush my fingertips across the top.

The plastic panel was smooth to the touch, and I carefully lifted the paper flap to pull the CD out of its sleeve. In the five years since Theo gave it to me, I haven't played it once. I could never bring myself to touch it, opting instead to slide it inside one of my books, and my heart twisted knots at the thought of playing it now. Nostalgia's familiar longing panged through my chest as I loaded it into the CD player and exhaled.

My forefinger pressed the play button.

I could feel the bass vibrate through the seats, a nervous laugh escaping through my lips that came out more like a strangled sob. The tempo was upbeat, and I moved my left palm to the door so I could press my palm flat against the speaker.

I sat like this for over an hour. An hour and sixteen songs pounding their rhythms against my hand, vibrating through my entire body, as I sat in the car with the stereo cranked all the way up. Tears poured down my cheeks while I sat rigid and unmoving, my hand still glued to the door even though the vibrations had long since stopped.

That's when I heard it.

CHAPTER 30

A voice crackled to life through the speakers of the car, the sound of it unfamiliar to my ears.

You see, two years ago I decided to take the plunge and got cochlear implants. I wanted to hear the ocean, the waves crashing against the shore in a cacophony of endless rhythm. I didn't want to be defined by my hearing - or my lack thereof - and, thanks to advances in technology, cochlear implants were more effective than ever before.

While some in the deaf community might have frowned upon my decision, in the end, it was *my* decision. It wasn't something forced upon me, it wasn't because I felt like I was broken and needed to be fixed or to fit in or some shit like that.

It was because I made a decision. I wanted to hear. I was tired of the world around me, and I decided that I wanted to see - and hear - it in a new light.

Being able to hear was a shock at first, especially because I had to learn to adapt to the slew of sounds thrown at me from all sides. It wasn't something you think about, really, how your brain identifies and filters sounds - attributing sources in a heartbeat, focusing in on one specific sound - especially when you exist in a noisy world where even in the so-called silence you are almost never truly without sound.

I learned all of that and more. I even learned to appreciate when I could turn it off. That was the nice thing about cochlear implants. Simply remove the external device, and boom. Deaf once more. Silence once more.

I loved that I could have it both ways.

Eventually, I learned not to jump at the sound of a car horn on the street, how to force my brain to tune out background noise at a restaurant so I could hear my friend speaking, how to go through every second of every day without gaping - awestruck - at every plane that buzzed overhead, at the tinkle of wind chimes in the breeze, at the whoosh of leaves rustling before a summer storm.

I knew it was Theo's voice the second I heard it, even though I'd never heard it before. It shot through every fiber of my being, and it sent my world crashing to a halt for the second time in five long years.

"Ava, ummm, I know you'll probably never hear this," the voice chuckled, causing goose bumps to ripple over my skin. "But I just...I wanted to say that I think you're perfect, and - well - I'm really glad I met you. You're the only person who sees more in me than my 'potential', as weird as that sounds. And...I think I'm falling in love with you."

That was it. That was the entire message. It was over before it started, and I jammed my finger against the rewind button to play it over and over again while hot tears poured down my burning cheeks. I sucked in a breath, the oxygen hitting my lungs like a thousand knives, as I struggled to breathe, to think, to do...anything.

Theo's voice. I heard Theo's voice. I'd spent five years learning and experiencing newness almost every day - from the sound of the espresso machine at the local coffee shop to the boom of a jet roaring through the sky above my head - all of those sounds you don't think about, the things you take for granted, they were all new to me.

This, however...this nearly shattered me. Every piece of my fragile heart, painstakingly glued back together after five years, cracked and threatened to fall apart once more.

Don't get me wrong. I knew this was going to be hard. I knew it would be emotional. After the last five years, I'd spent my time avoiding this - avoiding San Francisco - because it hurt too much. I spent my summer vacations working a shitty retail job, and I managed to convince my mom and brother to fly out to Boston for Christmas so I could avoid the trip.

I didn't want to avoid it anymore. The bruise in my chest that beat, day after day, screamed in protest, but I decided to let it.

I decided to let myself feel, mourn, and - hopefully - move on.

CHAPTER 31

"Are you okay?" Cora asked me, looping her arm through mine as we walked through the art gallery.

Countless bodies were pressed together, most of them carrying shimmering glasses of iridescent glasses of champagne while they shuffled from place to place. I recognized more faces than I expected - and more than I was comfortable with - as Cora steered me through the upscale crowd toward one of the bow-tie clad servers.

I nodded, smiling at the server as I took a glass of champagne and promptly emptied it. The server chuckled while I exchanged my empty glass for a fresh one.

"Right," Cora said, her eyebrow lifted. "Ava, you've been gone all afternoon. You were supposed to be here an hour ago."

I shrugged, "At least I'm here."

My best friend rolled her eyes, sipping her champagne before scanning the crowd. The turnout was better than expected, at least two hundred people crammed together in the upscale art gallery in a trendy San Francisco neighborhood. Stark white walls void of decoration stood between the artwork, while bright lights hung from the vaulted ceiling. It was ultra modern and minimalist, a little too stark for my taste, and I missed the cozy red brick of Boston.

"What do you think?" Cora smiled, gesturing with her champagne flute.

"I think I'm missing several hours of prime Netflix viewing."

She snorted, "Ava, you're a famous photographer hosting her first solo gallery exhibition. This is a big deal!"

"It's schmoozing," I replied, taking a drink of my champagne. "You know I suck at schmoozing."

Cora grinned, "Good thing they're the ones doing the schmoozing now that you're super famous. I mean, hell, you've got like three million followers on Instagram."

She pushed me forward, and I plastered a polite smile on my face. We passed her sister, Riya, and her new fiancé, a hugely famous action movie star, and I thanked them for coming. While half of the people here I hated, they were among the few whose support I actually appreciated.

Cora released her grip on my arm to say hi to someone from high school, and I used the opportunity to squeeze past several tipsy couples whilst pushing my way toward the front of the gallery. They didn't serve real food at these things, but I saw a server with a tray of chocolate near the front who I planned on stalking and relieving him of the burden of his entire tray.

Narrowly dodging a flying elbow, I pivoted to my left and came face to face with someone I never thought I'd see again. It was one of those moments like you see in the movies, except instead of dropping my glass of champagne, I had to fight the urge to chug the rest of it on the spot. My heart slammed against my ribcage like a jackhammer, each beat thrumming faster and faster, as I failed to find the words to speak.

Before I could try, the gallery owner grabbed my arm and pulled me after her. A boisterous redhead wearing outrageously high platform stilettos and a skin-tight black dress, she smiled sweetly - completely unaware of what she interrupted - as she pushed me toward the makeshift stage near the center of the gallery.

"Excuse me, everyone," she said, dropping my arm as she accepted the microphone from the DJ. "Thank you all for coming tonight. I'm so pleased with this exhibit, and it's *such* a pleasure to share Ava's work with all of you in such a personal and intimate way."

A few people clapped, and I flushed pink as I polished off the rest of my champagne before relinquishing it to a nearby waiter.

"Now, I know I could ramble on all night," the gallery owner simpered, earning a few hollow laughs. "But I know that's not what you're here for. So, without further ado, let me introduce to you, Ava Collins!"

She smiled at the applauding audience before waving me forward and thrust the microphone into my hands. A stab of panic flooded through me as I took it, and I forced myself to smile at the crowd.

"Thank you," I said, enunciating clearly. "Thank you for coming."

I waited for the crowd to settle, my fingers tightening on the microphone while my smile tightened as well.

"I'm not really one for public speaking, or - you know - *audible* speaking," I joked awkwardly, meeting

Cora's approving gaze, before continuing. "So, I'll try to keep this brief."

I scanned the crowd, and I regretted it a split second later when my eyes locked with the same pair I'd seen for the first time in five years less than two minutes earlier. The words caught in my throat, and I exhaled without breaking my gaze. After a moment, Theo's mom smiled - her chocolate brown eyes so similar to the ones forever seared into my memory, to the ones captured in so many of the photographs hanging throughout the gallery - and I nodded imperceptibly.

"As some of you know, the young man in many of these photographs is no longer with us," I said slowly. "His name was Theo."

A few people nodded, no doubt many remembering the tragic loss of an eighteen-year-old rising star, and I hesitated a moment before continuing.

"Unfortunately, five years ago Theo was in a car accident that took his life. He was hit by a drunk driver, and he died on impact."

My voice cracked, and I took a moment to wipe away the tears pooling in the corners of my eyes.

"I took these photographs in the weeks before he died, and I took the rest about six months ago. I realized that I'd been running away from him, from the pain and the loss, when - the truth of it is - I see him everywhere. I see him in all the same places. In the Observation Deck overlooking the ocean. In Lake Merced Park, staring at me from a rickety old picnic table. In the streets we walked together, in every second of every day, I see his smile."

I tried to smile, and I noticed Cora wiping away tears as she smiled back at me.

"That's what I wanted to capture with these photographs, and that's why I went back to the same places where I took the first ones," I said softly. "Even though Theo's gone, he's not...not really. He taught me so much about life. How to be a friend. How to fall in love. And now that he's gone...he taught me that it's okay to miss him. It's okay to hurt. Because, really, we're all a little bit broken. We just have to learn that we don't need to be fixed. We just need to be loved."

CPSIA information can be obtained
at www.ICGtesting.com
Printed in the USA
BVOW06s0235060717
488656BV00014B/151/P